Beowulf

In

Old English

And

New English

Facing Page Translation

J. H. Ford, Editor

F. B. Gummere, Translator

Beowulf
By Anonymous
Edited by James H. Ford
Translated by Francis B. Gummere

First Edition – July 2005

Published by
EL Paso Norte Press
404 Christopher Ave
El Paso, Texas 79912

ISBN 0-9760726-5-3

Printed in the United States of America

Beowulf

Preface

The importance of Beowulf cannot be overstated. Not only is it important as a historical link to the earliest days of English literature, as a linguistic resource of incalculable value and for the insight it provides into the ancient customs and mores of the Nordic peoples, but also, for its own sake, as very good literature.

The Old English language of Beowulf has a charm of its own, but it has become rather opaque through the passage of time. For this reason, a translation into New English is necessary for the story to be accessible to audiences of today. The question then arises as to how modern the language of the translation should be in order to transmit the tale with most of its original flavor intact; too old and it is still opaque, too new and it does not represent the essence of the tale.

Beowulf needs to be told, to be spoken aloud in a dramatic voice, to be appreciated in its fullest context. That is how those who first knew it came to appreciate the adventure, excitement and drama of the tale - sitting together, listening to a story-teller reciting the fantastic saga of Beowulf. The language of Francis Gummere's 19th century England bridges the gap from the original voice to the modern ear most admirably. That, however, should not be taken as an excuse to discard the original text. The richness of original cannot be replaced with an approximation.

The facing page translation presented in this volume offers the reader the opportunity to reach into the past in easy stages. The original does not lend itself to a rote mechanical translation given the inflected character of Old English. A sensible translation requires a deep insight into the character of the English language itself and the considerable literary skill that Gummere so aptly applied with a subtle hand.

Beowulf

Traveling back in time to touch ancient roots is, in itself, an important exercise for the human spirit. An aid, such as the New English translation presented here, is but a station on the journey and not the final destination. As much as any pilgrim might be in want of assistance, each must ultimately reach the destination in his or her own mind. The anonymous scribe who recorded the tale of Beowulf left, for posterity, a road map to a magnificent view of the past.

No education can be complete without taking a few such journeys. It is the intellectual span that Beowulf offers that marks it as a great work. The fullness, richness, range and depth are only accessible if you are willing and able to take the journey. Beowulf is a link, not only to the past, but among those who have traveled a common path. Among its many virtues, Beowulf touches the universal human need for things that are larger than life.

- J. H. Ford

Beowulf

Summary

The Beowulf poem opens with a few verses in praise of the Danish Kings, especially Scyld. His death is related, and his descendants briefly traced down to Hrothgar.

Hrothgar, elated with his prosperity and success in war, builds a magnificent hall, which he calls Heorot. In this hall Hrothgar and his retainers live in joy and festivity, until a malignant fiend, called Grendel, jealous of their happiness, carries off by night thirty of Hrothgar's men, and devours them in his moorland retreat. These ravages go on for twelve years.

Beowulf, a thane of Hygelac, King of the Goths, hearing of Hrothgar's calamities, sails from Sweden with fourteen warriors to help him. They reach the Danish coast in safety; and, after an animated parley with Hrothgar's coastguard, who at first takes them for pirates, they are allowed to proceed to the royal hall, where they are well received by Hrothgar.

A banquet ensues, during which Beowulf is taunted by the envious Hunferth about his swimming-match with Breca, King of the Brondings. Beowulf gives the true account of the contest, and silences Hunferth.

At night-fall the King departs, leaving Beowulf in charge of the hall. Grendel soon breaks in, seizes and devours one of Beowulf's companions; is attacked by Beowulf, and, after losing an arm, which is torn off by Beowulf, escapes to the fens. The joy of Hrothgar and the Danes, and their festivities, are described, various episodes are introduced, and Beowulf and his companions receive splendid gifts.

The next night Grendel's mother revenges her son by carrying off Aeschere, the friend and councilor of Hrothgar,

5

during the absence of Beowulf. Hrothgar appeals to Beowulf for vengeance, and describes the haunts of Grendel and his mother. They all proceed thither; the scenery of the lake, and the monsters that dwell in it, are described.

Beowulf plunges into the water, and attacks Grendel's mother in her dwelling at the bottom of the lake. He at length overcomes her, and cuts off her head, together with that of Grendel, and brings the heads to Hrothgar.

He then takes leave of Hrothgar, sails back to Sweden, and relates his adventures to Hygelac. Here the first half of the poem ends.

The second begins with the accession of Beowulf to the throne, after the fall of Hygelac and his son Heardred. He rules prosperously for fifty years, till a dragon, brooding over a hidden treasure, begins to ravage the country, and destroys Beowulf's palace with fire.

Beowulf sets out in quest of its hiding-place, with twelve men. Having a presentiment of his approaching end, he pauses and recalls to mind his past life and exploits. He then takes leave of his followers, one by one, and advances alone to attack the dragon. Unable, from the heat, to enter the cavern, he shouts aloud, and the dragon comes forth. The dragon's scaly hide is proof against Beowulf's sword, and he is reduced to great straits.

Then Wiglaf, one of his followers, advances to help him. Wiglaf's shield is consumed by the dragon's fiery breath, and he is compelled to seek shelter under Beowulf's shield of iron. Beowulf's sword snaps asunder, and he is seized by the dragon. Wiglaf stabs the dragon from underneath, and Beowulf cuts it in two with his dagger.

Beowulf

Feeling that his end is near, he bids Wiglaf bring out the treasures from the cavern, that he may see them before he dies. Wiglaf enters the dragon's den, which is described, returns to Beowulf, and receives his last commands.

Beowulf dies, and Wiglaf bitterly reproaches his companions for their cowardice. The disastrous consequences of Beowulf's death are then foretold, and the poem ends with his funeral.

-H. Sweet

Beowulf

Contents

Beowulf

Hwæt! We Gardena   in geardagum,
þeodcyninga,   þrym gefrunon,
hu ða æþelingas   ellen fremedon.
Oft Scyld Scefing   sceaþena þreatum,
5
monegum mægþum,   meodosetla ofteah,
egsode eorlas.   Syððan ærest wearð
feasceaft funden,   he þæs frofre gebad,
weox under wolcnum,   weorðmyndum þah,
oðþæt him æghwylc   þara ymbsittendra
10
ofer hronrade   hyran scolde,
gomban gyldan.   þæt wæs god cyning!
Ðæm eafera wæs   æfter cenned,
geong in geardum,   þone god sende
folce to frofre;   fyrenðearfe ongeat
15
þe hie ær drugon   aldorlease
lange hwile.   Him þæs liffrea,
wuldres wealdend,   woroldare forgeaf;
Beowulf wæs breme   (blæd wide sprang),
Scyldes eafera   Scedelandum in.
20
Swa sceal geong guma   gode gewyrcean,
fromum feohgiftum   on fæder bearme,
þæt hine on ylde   eft gewunigen
wilgesiþas,   þonne wig cume,
leode gelæsten;   lofdædum sceal
25
in mægþa gehwære   man geþeon.
Him ða Scyld gewat   to gescæphwile
felahror feran   on frean wære.
Hi hyne þa ætbæron   to brimes faroðe,
swæse gesiþas,   swa he selfa bæd,

30
þenden wordum weold   wine Scyldinga;
leof landfruma   lange ahte.
þær æt hyðe stod   hringedstefna,
isig ond utfus,   æþelinges fær.
Aledon þa   leofne þeoden,

I. THE PASSING OF SCYLD.

LO, praise of the prowess of people-kings
of spear-armed Danes, in days long sped,
we have heard, and what honor the athelings won!
Oft Scyld the Scefing from squadroned foes,
5
from many a tribe, the mead-bench tore,
awing the earls. Since erst he lay
friendless, a foundling, fate repaid him:
for he waxed under welkin, in wealth he throve,
till before him the folk, both far and near,
10
who house by the whale-path, heard his mandate,
gave him gifts: a good king he!
To him an heir was afterward born,
a son in his halls, whom heaven sent
to favor the folk, feeling their woe
15
that erst they had lacked an earl for leader
so long a while; the Lord endowed him,
the Wielder of Wonder, with world's renown.
Famed was this Beowulf: {1} far flew the boast of him,
son of Scyld, in the Scandian lands.
20
So becomes it a youth to quit him well
with his father's friends, by fee and gift,
that to aid him, aged, in after days,
come warriors willing, should war draw nigh,
liegemen loyal: by lauded deeds
25
shall an earl have honor in every clan.
Forth he fared at the fated moment,
sturdy Scyld to the shelter of God.
Then they bore him over to ocean's billow,
loving clansmen, as late he charged them,
30
while wielded words the winsome Scyld,
the leader beloved who long had ruled....
In the roadstead rocked a ring-dight vessel,
ice-flecked, outbound, atheling's barge:
there laid they down their darling lord

35
beaga bryttan,   on bearm scipes,
mærne be mæste.   þær wæs madma fela
of feorwegum,   frætwa, gelæded;
ne hyrde ic cymlicor   ceol gegyrwan
hildewæpnum   ond heaðowædum,
40
billum ond byrnum;   him on bearme læg
madma mænigo,   þa him mid scoldon
on flodes æht   feor gewitan.
Nalæs hi hine læssan   lacum teodan,
þeodgestreonum,   þon þa dydon
45
þe hine æt frumsceafte   forð onsendon
ænne ofer yðe   umborwesende.
þa gyt hie him asetton   segen geldenne
heah ofer heafod,   leton holm beran,
geafon on garsecg;   him wæs geomor sefa,
50
murnende mod.   Men ne cunnon
secgan to soðe,   selerædende,
hæleð under heofenum,   hwa þæm hlæste onfeng.

35
on the breast of the boat, the breaker-of-rings, {2}
by the mast the mighty one. Many a treasure
fetched from far was freighted with him.
No ship have I known so nobly dight
with weapons of war and weeds of battle,
40
with breastplate and blade: on his bosom lay
a heaped hoard that hence should go
far o'er the flood with him floating away.
No less these loaded the lordly gifts,
thanes' huge treasure, than those had done
45
who in former time forth had sent him
sole on the seas, a suckling child.
High o'er his head they hoist the standard,
a gold-wove banner; let billows take him,
gave him to ocean. Grave were their spirits,
50
mournful their mood. No man is able
to say in sooth, no son of the halls,
no hero 'neath heaven, -- who harbored that freight!

Ða wæs on burgum   Beowulf Scyldinga,
leof leodcyning,   longe þrage
55
folcum gefræge   (fæder ellor hwearf,
aldor of earde),   oþþæt him eft onwoc
heah Healfdene;   heold þenden lifde,
gamol ond guðreouw,   glæde Scyldingas.
ðæm feower bearn   forð gerimed
60
in worold wocun,   weoroda ræswan,
Heorogar ond Hroðgar   ond Halga til;
hyrde ic þæt   wæs Onelan cwen,
Heaðoscilfingas   healsgebedda.
þa wæs Hroðgare   heresped gyfen,
65
wiges weorðmynd,   þæt him his winemagas
georne hyrdon,   oðð þæt seo geogoð geweox,
magodriht micel.   Him on mod bearn
þæt healreced   hatan wolde,
medoærn micel,   men gewyrcean
70
þonne yldo bearn   æfre gefrunon,
ond þær on innan   eall gedælan
geongum ond ealdum,   swylc him god sealde,
buton folcscare   ond feorum gumena.
ða ic wide gefrægn   weorc gebannan
75
manigre mægþe   geond þisne middangeard,
folcstede frætwan.   Him on fyrste gelomp,
ædre mid yldum,   þæt hit wearð ealgearo,
healærna mæst;   scop him Heort naman
se þe his wordes geweald   wide hæfde.
80
He beot ne aleh,   beagas dælde,
sinc æt symle.   Sele hlifade,
heah ond horngeap,   heaðowylma bad,
laðan liges;   ne wæs hit lenge þa gen
þæt se ecghete   aþumsweorum
85
æfter wælniðe   wæcnan scolde.
ða se ellengæst   earfoðlice

II. THE HALL HEOROT.

Now Beowulf bode in the burg of the Scyldings,
leader beloved, and long he ruled
55
in fame with all folk, since his father had gone
away from the world, till awoke an heir,
haughty Healfdene, who held through life,
sage and sturdy, the Scyldings glad.
Then, one after one, there woke to him,
60
to the chieftain of clansmen, children four:
Heorogar, then Hrothgar, then Halga brave;
and I heard that -- was -- 's queen,
the Heathoscylfing's helpmate dear.
To Hrothgar was given such glory of war,
65
such honor of combat, that all his kin
obeyed him gladly till great grew his band
of youthful comrades. It came in his mind
to bid his henchmen a hall uprear,
a master mead-house, mightier far
70
than ever was seen by the sons of earth,
and within it, then, to old and young
he would all allot that the Lord had sent him,
save only the land and the lives of his men.
Wide, I heard, was the work commanded,
75
for many a tribe this mid-earth round,
to fashion the folkstead. It fell, as he ordered,
in rapid achievement that ready it stood there,
of halls the noblest: Heorot {3} he named it
whose message had might in many a land.
80
Not reckless of promise, the rings he dealt,
treasure at banquet: there towered the hall,
high, gabled wide, the hot surge waiting
of furious flame. {4} Nor far was that day
when father and son-in-law stood in feud
85
for warfare and hatred that woke again. {5}
With envy and anger an evil spirit

þrage geþolode,   se þe in þystrum bad,
þæt he dogora gehwam   dream gehyrde
hludne in healle;   þær wæs hearpan sweg,
90
swutol sang scopes.   Sægde se þe cuþe
frumsceaft fira   feorran reccan,
cwæð þæt se ælmihtiga   eorðan worhte,
wlitebeorhtne wang,   swa wæter bebugeð,
gesette sigehreþig   sunnan ond monan
95
leoman to leohte   landbuendum
ond gefrætwade   foldan sceatas
leomum ond leafum,   lif eac gesceop
cynna gehwylcum   þara ðe cwice hwyrfaþ.
Swa ða drihtguman   dreamum lifdon
100
eadiglice,   oððæt an ongan
fyrene fremman   feond on helle.
Wæs se grimma gæst   Grendel haten,
mære mearcstapa,   se þe moras heold,
fen ond fæsten;   fifelcynnes eard
105
wonsæli wer   weardode hwile,
siþðan him scyppend   forscrifen hæfde
in Caines cynne.   þone cwealm gewræc
ece drihten,   þæs þe he Abel slog;
ne gefeah he þære fæhðe,   ac he hine feor forwræc,
110
metod for þy mane,   mancynne fram.
þanon untydras   ealle onwocon,
eotenas ond ylfe   ond orcneas,
swylce gigantas,   þa wið gode wunnon
lange þrage;   he him ðæs lean forgeald.

endured the dole in his dark abode,
that he heard each day the din of revel
high in the hall: there harps rang out,
90
clear song of the singer. He sang who knew {6}
tales of the early time of man,
how the Almighty made the earth,
fairest fields enfolded by water,
set, triumphant, sun and moon
95
for a light to lighten the land-dwellers,
and braided bright the breast of earth
with limbs and leaves, made life for all
of mortal beings that breathe and move.
So lived the clansmen in cheer and revel
100
a winsome life, till one began
to fashion evils, that field of hell.
Grendel this monster grim was called,
march-riever {7} mighty, in moorland living,
in fen and fastness; fief of the giants
105
the hapless wight a while had kept
since the Creator his exile doomed.
On kin of Cain was the killing avenged
by sovran God for slaughtered Abel.
Ill fared his feud, {8} and far was he driven,
110
for the slaughter's sake, from sight of men.
Of Cain awoke all that woful breed,
Etins {9} and elves and evil-spirits,
as well as the giants that warred with God
weary while: but their wage was paid them!

115
Gewat ða neosian,   syþðan niht becom,
hean huses,   hu hit Hringdene
æfter beorþege   gebun hæfdon.
Fand þa ðær inne   æþelinga gedriht
swefan æfter symble;   sorge ne cuðon,
120
wonsceaft wera.   Wiht unhælo,
grim ond grædig,   gearo sona wæs,
reoc ond reþe,   ond on ræste genam
þritig þegna,   þanon eft gewat
huðe hremig   to ham faran,
125
mid þære wælfylle   wica neosan.
ða wæs on uhtan   mid ærdæge
Grendles guðcræft   gumum undyrne;
þa wæs æfter wiste   wop up ahafen,
micel morgensweg.   Mære þeoden,
130
æþeling ærgod,   unbliðe sæt,
þolode ðryðswyð,   þegnsorge dreah,
syðþan hie þæs laðan   last sceawedon,
wergan gastes;   wæs þæt gewin to strang,
lað ond longsum.   Næs hit lengra fyrst,
135
ac ymb ane niht   eft gefremede
morðbeala mare   ond no mearn fore,
fæhðe ond fyrene;   wæs to fæst on þam.
þa wæs eaðfynde   þe him elles hwær
gerumlicor   ræste sohte,
140
bed æfter burum,   ða him gebeacnod wæs,
gesægd soðlice   sweotolan tacne
healðegnes hete;   heold hyne syðþan
fyr ond fæstor   se þæm feonde ætwand.
Swa rixode   ond wið rihte wan,
145
ana wið eallum,   oðþæt idel stod
husa selest.   Wæs seo hwil micel;
XII wintra tid   torn geþolode

III. GRENDEL'S VISITS.

115
WENT he forth to find at fall of night
that haughty house, and heed wherever
the Ring-Danes, outrevelled, to rest had gone.
Found within it the atheling band
asleep after feasting and fearless of sorrow,
120
of human hardship. Unhallowed wight,
grim and greedy, he grasped betimes,
wrathful, reckless, from resting-places,
thirty of the thanes, and thence he rushed
fain of his fell spoil, faring homeward,
125
laden with slaughter, his lair to seek.
Then at the dawning, as day was breaking,
the might of Grendel to men was known;
then after wassail was wail uplifted,
loud moan in the morn. The mighty chief,
130
atheling excellent, unblithe sat,
labored in woe for the loss of his thanes,
when once had been traced the trail of the fiend,
spirit accurst: too cruel that sorrow,
too long, too loathsome. Not late the respite;
135
with night returning, anew began
ruthless murder; he recked no whit,
firm in his guilt, of the feud and crime.
They were easy to find who elsewhere sought
in room remote their rest at night,
140
bed in the bowers, {10} when that bale was shown,
was seen in sooth, with surest token, --
the hall-thane's {11} hate. Such held themselves
far and fast who the fiend outran!
Thus ruled unrighteous and raged his fill
145
one against all; until empty stood
that lordly building, and long it bode so.
Twelve years' tide the trouble he bore,

wine Scyldinga,   weana gehwelcne,
sidra sorga.   Forðam secgum wearð,
150
ylda bearnum,   undyrne cuð,
gyddum geomore,   þætte Grendel wan
hwile wið Hroþgar,   heteniðas wæg,
fyrene ond fæhðe   fela missera,
singale sæce,   sibbe ne wolde
155
wið manna hwone   mægenes Deniga,
feorhbealo feorran,   fea þingian,
ne þær nænig witena   wenan þorfte
beorhtre bote   to banan folmum,
ac se æglæca   ehtende wæs,
160
deorc deaþscua,   duguþe ond geogoþe,
seomade ond syrede,   sinnihte heold
mistige moras;   men ne cunnon
hwyder helrunan   hwyrftum scriþað.
Swa fela fyrena   feond mancynnes,
165
atol angengea,   oft gefremede,
heardra hynða.   Heorot eardode,
sincfage sel   sweartum nihtum;
no he þone gifstol   gretan moste,
maþðum for metode,   ne his myne wisse.
170
þæt wæs wræc micel   wine Scyldinga,
modes brecða.   Monig oft gesæt
rice to rune;   ræd eahtedon
hwæt swiðferhðum   selest wære
wið færgryrum   to gefremmanne.
175
Hwilum hie geheton   æt hærgtrafum
wigweorþunga,   wordum bædon
þæt him gastbona   geoce gefremede
wið þeodþreaum.   Swylc wæs þeaw hyra,
hæþenra hyht;   helle gemundon
180
in modsefan,   metod hie ne cuþon,
dæda demend,   ne wiston hie drihten god,
ne hie huru heofena helm   herian ne cuþon,
wuldres waldend.   Wa bið þæm ðe sceal

sovran of Scyldings, sorrows in plenty,
boundless cares. There came unhidden
150
tidings true to the tribes of men,
in sorrowful songs, how ceaselessly Grendel
harassed Hrothgar, what hate he bore him,
what murder and massacre, many a year,
feud unfading, -- refused consent
155
to deal with any of Daneland's earls,
make pact of peace, or compound for gold:
still less did the wise men ween to get
great fee for the feud from his fiendish hands.
But the evil one ambushed old and young
160
death-shadow dark, and dogged them still,
lured, or lurked in the livelong night
of misty moorlands: men may say not
where the haunts of these Hell-Runes {12} be.
Such heaping of horrors the hater of men,
165
lonely roamer, wrought unceasing,
harassings heavy. O'er Heorot he lorded,
gold-bright hall, in gloomy nights;
and ne'er could the prince {13} approach his throne,
-- 'twas judgment of God, -- or have joy in his hall.
170
Sore was the sorrow to Scyldings'-friend,
heart-rending misery. Many nobles
sat assembled, and searched out counsel
how it were best for bold-hearted men
against harassing terror to try their hand.
175
Whiles they vowed in their heathen fanes
altar-offerings, asked with words {14}
that the slayer-of-souls would succor give them
for the pain of their people. Their practice this,
their heathen hope; 'twas Hell they thought of
180
in mood of their mind. Almighty they knew not,
Doomsman of Deeds and dreadful Lord,
nor Heaven's-Helmet heeded they ever,
Wielder-of-Wonder. -- Woe for that man

þurh sliðne nið   sawle bescufan
185
in fyres fæþm,   frofre ne wenan,
wihte gewendan;   wel bið þæm þe mot
æfter deaðdæge   drihten secean
ond to fæder fæþmum   freoðo wilnian.

who in harm and hatred hales his soul
185
to fiery embraces; -- nor favor nor change
awaits he ever. But well for him
that after death-day may draw to his Lord,
and friendship find in the Father's arms!

Swa ða mælceare   maga Healfdenes
190
singala seað,   ne mihte snotor hæleð
wean onwendan;   wæs þæt gewin to swyð,
laþ ond longsum,   þe on ða leode becom,
nydwracu niþgrim,   nihtbealwa mæst.
þæt fram ham gefrægn   Higelaces þegn,
195
god mid Geatum,   Grendles dæda;
se wæs moncynnes   mægenes strengest
on þæm dæge   þysses lifes,
æþele ond eacen.   Het him yðlidan
godne gegyrwan,   cwæð, he guðcyning
200
ofer swanrade   secean wolde,
mærne þeoden,   þa him wæs manna þearf.
ðone siðfæt him   snotere ceorlas
lythwon logon,   þeah he him leof wære;
hwetton higerofne,   hæl sceawedon.
205
Hæfde se goda   Geata leoda
cempan gecorone   þara þe he cenoste
findan mihte;   XVna sum
sundwudu sohte;   secg wisade,
lagucræftig mon,   landgemyrcu.
210
Fyrst forð gewat.   Flota wæs on yðum,
bat under beorge.   Beornas gearwe
on stefn stigon;   streamas wundon,
sund wið sande;   secgas bæron
on bearm nacan   beorhte frætwe,
215
guðsearo geatolic;   guman ut scufon,
weras on wilsið,   wudu bundenne.
Gewat þa ofer wægholm,   winde gefysed,
flota famiheals   fugle gelicost,
oðþæt ymb antid   oþres dogores
220
wundenstefna   gewaden hæfde
þæt ða liðende   land gesawon,
brimclifu blican,   beorgas steape,

IV. HYGELAC'S THANE.

THUS seethed unceasing the son of Healfdene
190
with the woe of these days; not wisest men
assuaged his sorrow; too sore the anguish,
loathly and long, that lay on his folk,
most baneful of burdens and bales of the night.
This heard in his home Hygelac's thane,
195
great among Geats, of Grendel's doings.
He was the mightiest man of valor
in that same day of this our life,
stalwart and stately. A stout wave-walker
he bade make ready. Yon battle-king, said he,
200
far o'er the swan-road he fain would seek,
the noble monarch who needed men!
The prince's journey by prudent folk
was little blamed, though they loved him dear;
they whetted the hero, and hailed good omens.
205
And now the bold one from bands of Geats
comrades chose, the keenest of warriors
e'er he could find; with fourteen men
the sea-wood {15} he sought, and, sailor proved,
led them on to the land's confines.
210
Time had now flown; {16} afloat was the ship,
boat under bluff. On board they climbed,
warriors ready; waves were churning
sea with sand; the sailors bore
on the breast of the bark their bright array,
215
their mail and weapons: the men pushed off,
on its willing way, the well-braced craft.
Then moved o'er the waters by might of the wind
that bark like a bird with breast of foam,
till in season due, on the second day,
220
the curved prow such course had run
that sailors now could see the land,
sea-cliffs shining, steep high hills,

side sænæssas;   þa wæs sund liden,
eoletes æt ende.   þanon up hraðe
225
Wedera leode   on wang stigon,
sæwudu sældon   (syrcan hrysedon,
guðgewædo),   gode þancedon
þæs þe him yþlade   eaðe wurdon.
þa of wealle geseah   weard Scildinga,
230
se þe holmclifu   healdan scolde,
beran ofer bolcan   beorhte randas,
fyrdsearu fuslicu;   hine fyrwyt bræc
modgehygdum,   hwæt þa men wæron.
Gewat him þa to waroðe   wicge ridan
235
þegn Hroðgares,   þrymmum cwehte
mægenwudu mundum,   meþelwordum frægn:
"Hwæt syndon ge   searohæbbendra,
byrnum werede,   þe þus brontne ceol
ofer lagustræte   lædan cwomon,
240
hider ofer holmas?   ...le wæs
endesæta,   ægwearde heold,
þe on land Dena   laðra nænig
mid scipherge   sceðþan ne meahte.
No her cuðlicor   cuman ongunnon
245
lindhæbbende;   ne ge leafnesword
guðfremmendra   gearwe ne wisson,
maga gemedu.   Næfre ic maran geseah
eorla ofer eorþan   ðonne is eower sum,
secg on searwum;   nis þæt seldguma,
250
wæpnum geweorðad,   næfne him his wlite leoge,
ænlic ansyn.   Nu ic eower sceal
frumcyn witan,   ær ge fyr heonan,
leassceaweras,   on land Dena
furþur feran.   Nu ge feorbuend,
255
mereliðende,   minne gehyrað
anfealdne geþoht: Ofost is selest
to gecyðanne   hwanan eowre cyme syndon."

headlands broad. Their haven was found,
their journey ended. Up then quickly
225
the Weders' {17} clansmen climbed ashore,
anchored their sea-wood, with armor clashing
and gear of battle: God they thanked
or passing in peace o'er the paths of the sea.
Now saw from the cliff a Scylding clansman,
230
a warden that watched the water-side,
how they bore o'er the gangway glittering shields,
war-gear in readiness; wonder seized him
to know what manner of men they were.
Straight to the strand his steed he rode,
235
Hrothgar's henchman; with hand of might
he shook his spear, and spake in parley.
"Who are ye, then, ye armed men,
mailed folk, that yon mighty vessel
have urged thus over the ocean ways,
240
here o'er the waters? A warden I,
sentinel set o'er the sea-march here,
lest any foe to the folk of Danes
with harrying fleet should harm the land.
No aliens ever at ease thus bore them,
245
linden-wielders: {18} yet word-of-leave
clearly ye lack from clansmen here,
my folk's agreement. -- A greater ne'er saw I
of warriors in world than is one of you, --
yon hero in harness! No henchman he
250
worthied by weapons, if witness his features,
his peerless presence! I pray you, though, tell
your folk and home, lest hence ye fare
suspect to wander your way as spies
in Danish land. Now, dwellers afar,
255
ocean-travellers, take from me
simple advice: the sooner the better
I hear of the country whence ye came."

Him se yldesta   ondswarode,
werodes wisa,   wordhord onleac:
260
"We synt gumcynnes   Geata leode
ond Higelaces   heorðgeneatas.
Wæs min fæder   folcum gecyþed,
æþele ordfruma,   Ecgþeow haten.
Gebad wintra worn,   ær he on weg hwurfe,
265
gamol of geardum;   hine gearwe geman
witena welhwylc   wide geond eorþan.
We þurh holdne hige   hlaford þinne,
sunu Healfdenes,   secean cwomon,
leodgebyrgean;   wes þu us larena god.
270
Habbað we to þæm mæran   micel ærende,
Deniga frean,   ne sceal þær dyrne sum
wesan, þæs ic wene.   þu wast (gif hit is
swa we soþlice   secgan hyrdon)
þæt mid Scyldingum   sceaðona ic nat hwylc,
275
deogol dædhata,   deorcum nihtum
eaweð þurh egsan   uncuðne nið,
hynðu ond hrafyl.   Ic þæs Hroðgar mæg
þurh rumne sefan   ræd gelæran,
hu he frod ond god   feond oferswyðeþ,
280
gyf him edwendan   æfre scolde
bealuwa bisigu,   bot eft cuman,
ond þa cearwylmas   colran wurðaþ;
oððe a syþðan   earfoðþrage,
þreanyd þolað,   þenden þær wunað
285
on heahstede   husa selest."
Weard maþelode,   ðær on wicge sæt,
ombeht unforht: "æghwæþres sceal
scearp scyldwiga   gescad witan,
worda ond worca,   se þe wel þenceð.
290
Ic þæt gehyre,   þæt þis is hold weorod
frean Scyldinga.   Gewitaþ forð beran

V. THE ERRAND.

To him the stateliest spake in answer;
the warriors' leader his word-hoard unlocked: --
260
"We are by kin of the clan of Geats,
and Hygelac's own hearth-fellows we.
To folk afar was my father known,
noble atheling, Ecgtheow named.
Full of winters, he fared away
265
aged from earth; he is honored still
through width of the world by wise men all.
To thy lord and liege in loyal mood
we hasten hither, to Healfdene's son,
people-protector: be pleased to advise us!
270
To that mighty-one come we on mickle errand,
to the lord of the Danes; nor deem I right
that aught be hidden. We hear -- thou knowest
if sooth it is -- the saying of men,
that amid the Scyldings a scathing monster,
275
dark ill-doer, in dusky nights
shows terrific his rage unmatched,
hatred and murder. To Hrothgar I
in greatness of soul would succor bring,
so the Wise-and-Brave {19} may worst his foes, --
280
if ever the end of ills is fated,
of cruel contest, if cure shall follow,
and the boiling care-waves cooler grow;
else ever afterward anguish-days
he shall suffer in sorrow while stands in place
285
high on its hill that house unpeered!"
Astride his steed, the strand-ward answered,
clansman unquailing: "The keen-souled thane
must be skilled to sever and sunder duly
words and works, if he well intends.
290
I gather, this band is graciously bent
to the Scyldings' master. March, then, bearing

wæpen ond gewædu;   ic eow wisige.
Swylce ic maguþegnas   mine hate
wið feonda gehwone   flotan eowerne,
295
niwtyrwydne   nacan on sande
arum healdan,   oþðæt eft byreð
ofer lagustreamas   leofne mannan
wudu wundenhals   to Wedermearce,
godfremmendra   swylcum gifeþe bið
300
þæt þone hilderæs   hal gedigeð."
Gewiton him þa feran.   Flota stille bad,
seomode on sale   sidfæþmed scip,
on ancre fæst.   Eoforlic scionon
ofer hleorberan   gehroden golde,
305
fah ond fyrheard;   ferhwearde heold
guþmod grimmon.   Guman onetton,
sigon ætsomne,   oþþæt hy sæl timbred,
geatolic ond goldfah,   ongyton mihton;
þæt wæs foremærost   foldbuendum
310
receda under roderum,   on þæm se rica bad;
lixte se leoma   ofer landa fela.
Him þa hildedeor   hof modigra
torht getæhte,   þæt hie him to mihton
gegnum gangan;   guðbeorna sum
315
wicg gewende,   word æfter cwæð:
"Mæl is me to feran;   fæder alwalda
mid arstafum   eowic gehealde
siða gesunde.   Ic to sæ wille
wið wrað werod   wearde healdan."

weapons and weeds the way I show you.
I will bid my men your boat meanwhile
to guard for fear lest foemen come, --
295
your new-tarred ship by shore of ocean
faithfully watching till once again
it waft o'er the waters those well-loved thanes,
-- winding-neck'd wood, -- to Weders' bounds,
heroes such as the hest of fate
300
shall succor and save from the shock of war."
They bent them to march, -- the boat lay still,
fettered by cable and fast at anchor,
broad-bosomed ship. -- Then shone the boars {20}
over the cheek-guard; chased with gold,
305
keen and gleaming, guard it kept
o'er the man of war, as marched along
heroes in haste, till the hall they saw,
broad of gable and bright with gold:
that was the fairest, 'mid folk of earth,
310
of houses 'neath heaven, where Hrothgar lived,
and the gleam of it lightened o'er lands afar.
The sturdy shieldsman showed that bright
burg-of-the-boldest; bade them go
straightway thither; his steed then turned,
315
hardy hero, and hailed them thus: --
"'Tis time that I fare from you. Father Almighty
in grace and mercy guard you well,
safe in your seekings. Seaward I go,
'gainst hostile warriors hold my watch."

320
Stræt wæs stanfah,   stig wisode
gumum ætgædere.   Guðbyrne scan
heard hondlocen,   hringiren scir
song in searwum,   þa hie to sele furðum
in hyra gryregeatwum   gangan cwomon.
325
Setton sæmeþe   side scyldas,
rondas regnhearde,   wið þæs recedes weal,
bugon þa to bence.   Byrnan hringdon,
guðsearo gumena;   garas stodon,
sæmanna searo,   samod ætgædere,
330
æscholt ufan græg;   wæs se irenþreat
wæpnum gewurþad.   þa ðær wlonc hæleð
oretmecgas   æfter æþelum frægn:
"Hwanon ferigeað ge   fætte scyldas,
græge syrcan   ond grimhelmas,
335
heresceafta heap?   Ic eom Hroðgares
ar ond ombiht.   Ne seah ic elþeodige
þus manige men   modiglicran.
Wen ic þæt ge for wlenco,   nalles for wræcsiðum,
ac for higeþrymmum   Hroðgar sohton."
340
Him þa ellenrof   andswarode,
wlanc Wedera leod,   word æfter spræc,
heard under helme: "We synt Higelaces
beodgeneatas;   Beowulf is min nama.
Wille ic asecgan   sunu Healfdenes,
345
mærum þeodne,   min ærende,
aldre þinum,   gif he us geunnan wile
þæt we hine swa godne   gretan moton."
Wulfgar maþelode   (þæt wæs Wendla leod;
wæs his modsefa   manegum gecyðed,
350
wig ond wisdom):   "Ic þæs wine Deniga,
frean Scildinga,   frinan wille,
beaga bryttan,   swa þu bena eart,

VI. BEOWULF'S SPEECH.

320
STONE-BRIGHT the street: {21} it showed the way
to the crowd of clansmen. Corselets glistened
hand-forged, hard; on their harness bright
the steel ring sang, as they strode along
in mail of battle, and marched to the hall.
325
There, weary of ocean, the wall along
they set their bucklers, their broad shields, down,
and bowed them to bench: the breastplates clanged,
war-gear of men; their weapons stacked,
spears of the seafarers stood together,
330
gray-tipped ash: that iron band
was worthily weaponed! -- A warrior proud
asked of the heroes their home and kin.
"Whence, now, bear ye burnished shields,
harness gray and helmets grim,
335
spears in multitude? Messenger, I,
Hrothgar's herald! Heroes so many
ne'er met I as strangers of mood so strong.
'Tis plain that for prowess, not plunged into exile,
for high-hearted valor, Hrothgar ye seek!"
340
Him the sturdy-in-war bespake with words,
proud earl of the Weders answer made,
hardy 'neath helmet: -- "Hygelac's, we,
fellows at board; I am Beowulf named.
I am seeking to say to the son of Healfdene
345
this mission of mine, to thy master-lord,
the doughty prince, if he deign at all
grace that we greet him, the good one, now."
Wulfgar spake, the Wendles' chieftain,
whose might of mind to many was known,
350
his courage and counsel: "The king of Danes,
the Scyldings' friend, I fain will tell,
the Breaker-of-Rings, as the boon thou askest,

þeoden mærne, ymb þinne sið,
ond þe þa ondsware ædre gecyðan
355
ðe me se goda agifan þenceð."
Hwearf þa hrædlice þær Hroðgar sæt
eald ond anhar mid his eorla gedriht;
eode ellenrof, þæt he for eaxlum gestod
Deniga frean; cuþe he duguðe þeaw.
360
Wulfgar maðelode to his winedrihtne:
"Her syndon geferede, feorran cumene
ofer geofenes begang Geata leode;
þone yldestan oretmecgas
Beowulf nemnað. Hy benan synt
365
þæt hie, þeoden min, wið þe moton
wordum wrixlan. No ðu him wearne geteoh
ðinra gegncwida, glædman Hroðgar.
Hy on wiggetawum wyrðe þinceað
eorla geæhtlan; huru se aldor deah,
370
se þæm heaðorincum hider wisade."

the famed prince, of thy faring hither,
and, swiftly after, such answer bring
355
as the doughty monarch may deign to give."
Hied then in haste to where Hrothgar sat
white-haired and old, his earls about him,
till the stout thane stood at the shoulder there
of the Danish king: good courtier he!
360
Wulfgar spake to his winsome lord: --
"Hither have fared to thee far-come men
o'er the paths of ocean, people of Geatland;
and the stateliest there by his sturdy band
is Beowulf named. This boon they seek,
365
that they, my master, may with thee
have speech at will: nor spurn their prayer
to give them hearing, gracious Hrothgar!
In weeds of the warrior worthy they,
methinks, of our liking; their leader most surely,
370
a hero that hither his henchmen has led."

Hroðgar maþelode,   helm Scyldinga:
"Ic hine cuðe   cnihtwesende.
Wæs his ealdfæder   Ecgþeo haten,
ðæm to ham forgeaf   Hreþel Geata
375
angan dohtor;   is his eafora nu
heard her cumen,   sohte holdne wine.
ðonne sægdon þæt   sæliþende,
þa ðe gifsceattas   Geata fyredon
þyder to þance,   þæt he XXXtiges
380
manna mægencræft   on his mundgripe
heaþorof hæbbe.   Hine halig god
for arstafum   us onsende,
to Westdenum,   þæs ic wen hæbbe,
wið Grendles gryre.   Ic þæm godan sceal
385
for his modþræce   madmas beodan.
Beo ðu on ofeste,   hat in gan
seon sibbegedriht   samod ætgædere;
gesaga him eac wordum   þæt hie sint wilcuman
Deniga leodum."
390
    word inne abead:
"Eow het secgan   sigedrihten min,
aldor Eastdena,   þæt he eower æþelu can,
ond ge him syndon   ofer sæwylmas
heardhicgende   hider wilcuman.
395
Nu ge moton gangan   in eowrum guðgewædum
under heregriman   Hroðgar geseon;
lætað hildebord   her onbidan,
wudu, wælsceaftas,   worda geþinges."
Aras þa se rica,   ymb hine rinc manig,
400
þryðlic þegna heap;   sume þær bidon,
heaðoreaf heoldon,   swa him se hearda bebead.
Snyredon ætsomne,   þa secg wisode,
under Heorotes hrof

VII. HROTHGAR'S WELCOME.

HROTHGAR answered, helmet of Scyldings: --
"I knew him of yore in his youthful days;
his aged father was Ecgtheow named,
to whom, at home, gave Hrethel the Geat
375
his only daughter. Their offspring bold
fares hither to seek the steadfast friend.
And seamen, too, have said me this, --
who carried my gifts to the Geatish court,
thither for thanks, -- he has thirty men's
380
heft of grasp in the gripe of his hand,
the bold-in-battle. Blessed God
out of his mercy this man hath sent
to Danes of the West, as I ween indeed,
against horror of Grendel. I hope to give
385
the good youth gold for his gallant thought.
Be thou in haste, and bid them hither,
clan of kinsmen, to come before me;
and add this word, -- they are welcome guests
to folk of the Danes."
[To the door of the hall
390
Wulfgar went] and the word declared: --
"To you this message my master sends,
East-Danes' king, that your kin he knows,
hardy heroes, and hails you all
welcome hither o'er waves of the sea!
395
Ye may wend your way in war-attire,
and under helmets Hrothgar greet;
but let here the battle-shields bide your parley,
and wooden war-shafts wait its end."
Uprose the mighty one, ringed with his men,
400
brave band of thanes: some bode without,
battle-gear guarding, as bade the chief.
Then hied that troop where the herald led them,
under Heorot's roof: [the hero strode,]

heard under helme,   þæt he on heoðe gestod.
405
Beowulf maðelode   (on him byrne scan,
searonet seowed   smiþes orþancum):
"Wæs þu, Hroðgar, hal!   Ic eom Higelaces
mæg ond magoðegn;   hæbbe ic mærða fela
ongunnen on geogoþe.   Me wearð Grendles þing
410
on minre eþeltyrf   undyrne cuð;
secgað sæliðend   þæt þæs sele stande,
reced selesta,   rinca gehwylcum
idel ond unnyt,   siððan æfenleoht
under heofenes hador   beholen weorþeð.
415
þa me þæt gelærdon   leode mine
þa selestan,   snotere ceorlas,
þeoden Hroðgar,   þæt ic þe sohte,
forþan hie mægenes cræft   minne cuþon,
selfe ofersawon,   ða ic of searwum cwom,
420
fah from feondum,   þær ic fife geband,
yðde eotena cyn   ond on yðum slog
niceras nihtes,   nearoþearfe dreah,
wræc Wedera nið   (wean ahsodon),
forgrand gramum,   ond nu wið Grendel sceal,
425
wið þam aglæcan,   ana gehegan
ðing wið þyrse.   Ic þe nu ða,
brego Beorhtdena,   biddan wille,
eodor Scyldinga,   anre bene,
þæt ðu me ne forwyrne,   wigendra hleo,
430
freowine folca,   nu ic þus feorran com,
þæt ic mote ana   ond minra eorla gedryht,
þes hearda heap,   Heorot fælsian.
Hæbbe ic eac geahsod   þæt se æglæca
for his wonhydum   wæpna ne recceð.
435
Ic þæt þonne forhicge   (swa me Higelac sie,
min mondrihten,   modes bliðe),
þæt ic sweord bere   oþðe sidne scyld,
geolorand to guþe,   ac ic mid grape sceal
fon wið feonde   ond ymb feorh sacan,

hardy 'neath helm, till the hearth he neared.
405
Beowulf spake, -- his breastplate gleamed,
war-net woven by wit of the smith: --
"Thou Hrothgar, hail! Hygelac's I,
kinsman and follower. Fame a plenty
have I gained in youth! These Grendel-deeds
410
I heard in my home-land heralded clear.
Seafarers say how stands this hall,
of buildings best, for your band of thanes
empty and idle, when evening sun
in the harbor of heaven is hidden away.
415
So my vassals advised me well, --
brave and wise, the best of men, --
O sovran Hrothgar, to seek thee here,
for my nerve and my might they knew full well.
Themselves had seen me from slaughter come
420
blood-flecked from foes, where five I bound,
and that wild brood worsted. I' the waves I slew
nicors {22} by night, in need and peril
avenging the Weders, {23} whose woe they sought, --
crushing the grim ones. Grendel now,
425
monster cruel, be mine to quell
in single battle! So, from thee,
thou sovran of the Shining-Danes,
Scyldings'-bulwark, a boon I seek, --
and, Friend-of-the-folk, refuse it not,
430
O Warriors'-shield, now I've wandered far, --
that I alone with my liegemen here,
this hardy band, may Heorot purge!
More I hear, that the monster dire,
in his wanton mood, of weapons recks not;
435
hence shall I scorn -- so Hygelac stay,
king of my kindred, kind to me! --
brand or buckler to bear in the fight,
gold-colored targe: but with gripe alone
must I front the fiend and fight for life,

440
lað wið laþum;   ðær gelyfan sceal
dryhtnes dome   se þe hine deað nimeð.
Wen ic þæt he wille,   gif he wealdan mot,
in þæm guðsele   Geotena leode
etan unforhte,   swa he oft dyde,
445
mægen Hreðmanna.   Na þu minne þearft
hafalan hydan,   ac he me habban wile
dreore fahne,   gif mec deað nimeð.
Byreð blodig wæl,   byrgean þenceð,
eteð angenga   unmurnlice,
450
mearcað morhopu;   no ðu ymb mines ne þearft
lices feorme   leng sorgian.
Onsend Higelace,   gif mec hild nime,
beaduscruda betst,   þæt mine breost wereð,
hrægla selest;   þæt is Hrædlan laf,
455
Welandes geweorc.   Gæð a wyrd swa hio scel."

440
foe against foe. Then faith be his
in the doom of the Lord whom death shall take.
Fain, I ween, if the fight he win,
in this hall of gold my Geatish band
will he fearless eat, -- as oft before, --
445
my noblest thanes. Nor need'st thou then
to hide my head; {24} for his shall I be,
dyed in gore, if death must take me;
and my blood-covered body he'll bear as prey,
ruthless devour it, the roamer-lonely,
450
with my life-blood redden his lair in the fen:
no further for me need'st food prepare!
To Hygelac send, if Hild {25} should take me,
best of war-weeds, warding my breast,
armor excellent, heirloom of Hrethel
455
and work of Wayland. {26} Fares Wyrd {27} as she must."

Hroðgar maþelode,   helm Scyldinga:
"For gewyrhtum þu,   wine min Beowulf,
ond for arstafum   usic sohtest.
Gesloh þin fæder   fæhðe mæste;
460
wearþ he Heaþolafe   to handbonan
mid Wilfingum;   ða hine Wedera cyn
for herebrogan   habban ne mihte.
þanon he gesohte   Suðdena folc
ofer yða gewealc,   Arscyldinga.
465
ða ic furþum weold   folce Deniga
ond on geogoðe heold   ginne rice,
hordburh hæleþa;   ða wæs Heregar dead,
min yldra mæg   unlifigende,
bearn Healfdenes;   se wæs betera ðonne ic.
470
Siððan þa fæhðe   feo þingode;
sende ic Wylfingum   ofer wæteres hrycg
ealde madmas;   he me aþas swor.
Sorh is me to secganne   on sefan minum
gumena ængum   hwæt me Grendel hafað
475
hynðo on Heorote   mid his heteþancum,
færniða gefremed.   Is min fletwerod,
wigheap gewanod;   hie wyrd forsweop
on Grendles gryre.   God eaþe mæg
þone dolsceaðan   dæda getwæfan.
480
Ful oft gebeotedon   beore druncne
ofer ealowæge   oretmecgas
þæt hie in beorsele   bidan woldon
Grendles guþe   mid gryrum ecga.
ðonne wæs þeos medoheal   on morgentid,
485
drihtsele dreorfah,   þonne dæg lixte,
eal bencþelu   blode bestymed,
heall heorudreore;   ahte ic holdra þy læs,
deorre duguðe,   þe þa deað fornam.

VIII. HROTHGAR TELLS OF GRENDEL.

HROTHGAR spake, the Scyldings'-helmet: --
"For fight defensive, Friend my Beowulf,
to succor and save, thou hast sought us here.
Thy father's combat {28} a feud enkindled
460
when Heatholaf with hand he slew
among the Wylfings; his Weder kin
for horror of fighting feared to hold him.
Fleeing, he sought our South-Dane folk,
over surge of ocean the Honor-Scyldings,
465
when first I was ruling the folk of Danes,
wielded, youthful, this widespread realm,
this hoard-hold of heroes. Heorogar was dead,
my elder brother, had breathed his last,
Healfdene's bairn: he was better than I!
470
Straightway the feud with fee {29} I settled,
to the Wylfings sent, o'er watery ridges,
treasures olden: oaths he {30} swore me.
Sore is my soul to say to any
of the race of man what ruth for me
475
in Heorot Grendel with hate hath wrought,
what sudden harryings. Hall-folk fail me,
my warriors wane; for Wyrd hath swept them
into Grendel's grasp. But God is able
this deadly foe from his deeds to turn!
480
Boasted full oft, as my beer they drank,
earls o'er the ale-cup, armed men,
that they would bide in the beer-hall here,
Grendel's attack with terror of blades.
Then was this mead-house at morning tide
485
dyed with gore, when the daylight broke,
all the boards of the benches blood-besprinkled,
gory the hall: I had heroes the less,
doughty dear-ones that death had reft.
-- But sit to the banquet, unbind thy words,

Site nu to symle   ond onsæl meoto,
490
sigehreð secgum,   swa þin sefa hwette."
þa wæs Geatmæcgum   geador ætsomne
on beorsele   benc gerymed;
þær swiðferhþe   sittan eodon,
þryðum dealle.   þegn nytte beheold,
495
se þe on handa bær   hroden ealowæge,
scencte scir wered.   Scop hwilum sang
hador on Heorote.   þær wæs hæleða dream,
duguð unlytel   Dena ond Wedera.

490
hardy hero, as heart shall prompt thee."
Gathered together, the Geatish men
in the banquet-hall on bench assigned,
sturdy-spirited, sat them down,
hardy-hearted. A henchman attended,
495
carried the carven cup in hand,
served the clear mead. Oft minstrels sang
blithe in Heorot. Heroes revelled,
no dearth of warriors, Weder and Dane.

Unferð maþelode,   Ecglafes bearn,
500
þe æt fotum sæt   frean Scyldinga,
onband beadurune   (wæs him Beowulfes sið,
modges merefaran,   micel æfþunca,
forþon þe he ne uþe   þæt ænig oðer man
æfre mærða þon ma   middangeardes
505
gehedde under heofenum   þonne he sylfa):
"Eart þu se Beowulf,   se þe wið Brecan wunne,
on sidne sæ   ymb sund flite,
ðær git for wlence   wada cunnedon
ond for dolgilpe   on deop wæter
510
aldrum neþdon?   Ne inc ænig mon,
ne leof ne lað,   belean mihte
sorhfullne sið,   þa git on sund reon.
þær git eagorstream   earmum þehton,
mæton merestræta,   mundum brugdon,
515
glidon ofer garsecg;   geofon yþum weol,
wintrys wylmum.   Git on wæteres æht
seofon niht swuncon;   he þe æt sunde oferflat,
hæfde mare mægen.   þa hine on morgentid
on Heaþoræmas   holm up ætbær;
520
ðonon he gesohte   swæsne ,
leof his leodum,   lond Brondinga,
freoðoburh fægere,   þær he folc ahte,
burh ond beagas.   Beot eal wið þe
sunu Beanstanes   soðe gelæste.
525
ðonne wene ic to þe   wyrsan geþingea,
ðeah þu heaðoræsa   gehwær dohte,
grimre guðe,   gif þu Grendles dearst
nihtlongne fyrst   nean bidan."
Beowulf maþelode,   bearn Ecgþeowes:
530
"Hwæt! þu worn fela,   wine min Unferð,
beore druncen   ymb Brecan spræce,

IX. HUNFERTH OBJECTS TO BEOWULF.

UNFERTH spake, the son of Ecglaf,
500
who sat at the feet of the Scyldings' lord,
unbound the battle-runes. {31} -- Beowulf's quest,
sturdy seafarer's, sorely galled him;
ever he envied that other men
should more achieve in middle-earth
505
of fame under heaven than he himself. --
"Art thou that Beowulf, Breca's rival,
who emulous swam on the open sea,
when for pride the pair of you proved the floods,
and wantonly dared in waters deep
510
to risk your lives? No living man,
or lief or loath, from your labor dire
could you dissuade, from swimming the main.
Ocean-tides with your arms ye covered,
with strenuous hands the sea-streets measured,
515
swam o'er the waters. Winter's storm
rolled the rough waves. In realm of sea
a sennight strove ye. In swimming he topped thee,
had more of main! Him at morning-tide
billows bore to the Battling Reamas,
520
whence he hied to his home so dear
beloved of his liegemen, to land of Brondings,
fastness fair, where his folk he ruled,
town and treasure. In triumph o'er thee
Beanstan's bairn {32} his boast achieved.
525
So ween I for thee a worse adventure
-- though in buffet of battle thou brave hast been,
in struggle grim, -- if Grendel's approach
thou darst await through the watch of night!"

Beowulf spake, bairn of Ecgtheow: --
530
"What a deal hast uttered, dear my Unferth,
drunken with beer, of Breca now,

sægdest from his siðe.   Soð ic talige,
þæt ic merestrengo   maran ahte,
earfeþo on yþum,   ðonne ænig oþer man.
535
Wit þæt gecwædon   cnihtwesende
ond gebeotedon   (wæron begen þa git
on geogoðfeore)   þæt wit on garsecg ut
aldrum neðdon,   ond þæt geæfndon swa.
Hæfdon swurd nacod,   þa wit on sund reon,
540
heard on handa;   wit unc wið hronfixas
werian þohton.   No he wiht fram me
flodyþum feor   fleotan meahte,
hraþor on holme;   no ic fram him wolde.
ða wit ætsomne   on sæ wæron
545
fif nihta fyrst,   oþþæt unc flod todraf,
wado weallende,   wedera cealdost,
nipende niht,   ond norþanwind
heaðogrim ondhwearf;   hreo wæron yþa.
Wæs merefixa   mod onhrered;
550
þær me wið laðum   licsyrce min,
heard, hondlocen,   helpe gefremede,
beadohrægl broden   on breostum læg
golde gegyrwed.   Me to grunde teah
fah feondscaða,   fæste hæfde
555
grim on grape;   hwæþre me gyfeþe wearð
þæt ic aglæcan   orde geræhte,
hildebille;   heaþoræs fornam
mihtig meredeor   þurh mine hand.

told of his triumph! Truth I claim it,
that I had more of might in the sea
than any man else, more ocean-endurance.
535
We twain had talked, in time of youth,
and made our boast, -- we were merely boys,
striplings still, -- to stake our lives
far at sea: and so we performed it.
Naked swords, as we swam along,
540
we held in hand, with hope to guard us
against the whales. Not a whit from me
could he float afar o'er the flood of waves,
haste o'er the billows; nor him I abandoned.
Together we twain on the tides abode
545
five nights full till the flood divided us,
churning waves and chillest weather,
darkling night, and the northern wind
ruthless rushed on us: rough was the surge.
Now the wrath of the sea-fish rose apace;
550
yet me 'gainst the monsters my mailed coat,
hard and hand-linked, help afforded, --
battle-sark braided my breast to ward,
garnished with gold. There grasped me firm
and haled me to bottom the hated foe,
555
with grimmest gripe. 'Twas granted me, though,
to pierce the monster with point of sword,
with blade of battle: huge beast of the sea
was whelmed by the hurly through hand of mine.

Swa mec gelome   laðgeteonan
560
þreatedon þearle.   Ic him þenode
deoran sweorde,   swa hit gedefe wæs.
Næs hie ðære fylle   gefean hæfdon,
manfordædlan,   þæt hie me þegon,
symbel ymbsæton   sægrunde neah;
565
ac on mergenne   mecum wunde
be yðlafe   uppe lægon,
sweordum aswefede,   þæt syðþan na
ymb brontne ford   brimliðende
lade ne letton.   Leoht eastan com,
570
beorht beacen godes;   brimu swaþredon,
þæt ic sænæssas   geseon mihte,
windige weallas.   Wyrd oft nereð
unfægne eorl,   þonne his ellen deah.
Hwæþere me gesælde   þæt ic mid sweorde ofsloh
575
niceras nigene.   No ic on niht gefrægn
under heofones hwealf   heardran feohtan,
ne on egstreamum   earmran mannon;
hwaþere ic fara feng   feore gedigde,
siþes werig.   ða mec sæ oþbær,
580
flod æfter faroðe   on Finna land,
wadu weallendu.   No ic wiht fram þe
swylcra searoniða   secgan hyrde,
billa brogan.   Breca næfre git
æt heaðolace,   ne gehwæþer incer,
585
swa deorlice   dæd gefremede
fagum sweordum   (no ic þæs fela gylpe),
þeah ðu þinum broðrum   to banan wurde,
heafodmægum;   þæs þu in helle scealt
werhðo dreogan,   þeah þin wit duge.
590
Secge ic þe to soðe,   sunu Ecglafes,
þæt næfre Grendel swa fela   gryra gefremede,

X. BEOWULF'S CONTEST WITH BRECA.
-THE FEAST.

ME thus often the evil monsters
560
thronging threatened. With thrust of my sword,
the darling, I dealt them due return!
Nowise had they bliss from their booty then
to devour their victim, vengeful creatures,
seated to banquet at bottom of sea;
565
but at break of day, by my brand sore hurt,
on the edge of ocean up they lay,
put to sleep by the sword. And since, by them
on the fathomless sea-ways sailor-folk
are never molested. -- Light from east,
570
came bright God's beacon; the billows sank,
so that I saw the sea-cliffs high,
windy walls. For Wyrd oft saveth
earl undoomed if he doughty be!
And so it came that I killed with my sword
575
nine of the nicors. Of night-fought battles
ne'er heard I a harder 'neath heaven's dome,
nor adrift on the deep a more desolate man!
Yet I came unharmed from that hostile clutch,
though spent with swimming. The sea upbore me,
580
flood of the tide, on Finnish land,
the welling waters. No wise of thee
have I heard men tell such terror of falchions,
bitter battle. Breca ne'er yet,
not one of you pair, in the play of war
585
such daring deed has done at all
with bloody brand, -- I boast not of it! --
though thou wast the bane {33} of thy brethren dear,
thy closest kin, whence curse of hell
awaits thee, well as thy wit may serve!
590
For I say in sooth, thou son of Ecglaf,
never had Grendel these grim deeds wrought,

atol æglæca,   ealdre þinum,
hynðo on Heorote,   gif þin hige wære,
sefa swa searogrim,   swa þu self talast.
595
Ac he hafað onfunden   þæt he þa fæhðe ne þearf,
atole ecgþræce   eower leode
swiðe onsittan,   Sigescyldinga;
nymeð nydbade,   nænegum arað
leode Deniga,   ac he lust wigeð,
600
swefeð ond sendeþ,   secce ne weneþ
to Gardenum.   Ac ic him Geata sceal
eafoð ond ellen   ungeara nu,
guþe gebeodan.   Gæþ eft se þe mot
to medo modig,   siþþan morgenleoht
605
ofer ylda bearn   oþres dogores,
sunne sweglwered   suþan scineð."
þa wæs on salum   sinces brytta,
gamolfeax ond guðrof;   geoce gelyfde
brego Beorhtdena,   gehyrde on Beowulfe
610
folces hyrde   fæstrædne geþoht.
ðær wæs hæleþa hleahtor,   hlyn swynsode,
word wæron wynsume.   Eode Wealhþeow forð,
cwen Hroðgares,   cynna gemyndig,
grette goldhroden   guman on healle,
615
ond þa freolic wif   ful gesealde
ærest Eastdena   eþelwearde,
bæd hine bliðne   æt þære beorþege,
leodum leofne.   He on lust geþeah
symbel ond seleful,   sigerof kyning.
620
Ymbeode þa   ides Helminga
duguþe ond geogoþe   dæl æghwylcne,
sincfato sealde,   oþþæt sæl alamp
þæt hio Beowulfe,   beaghroden cwen
mode geþungen,   medoful ætbær;
625
grette Geata leod,   gode þancode
wisfæst wordum   þæs ðe hire se willa gelamp
þæt heo on ænigne   eorl gelyfde

monster dire, on thy master dear,
in Heorot such havoc, if heart of thine
were as battle-bold as thy boast is loud!
595
But he has found no feud will happen;
from sword-clash dread of your Danish clan
he vaunts him safe, from the Victor-Scyldings.
He forces pledges, favors none
of the land of Danes, but lustily murders,
600
fights and feasts, nor feud he dreads
from Spear-Dane men. But speedily now
shall I prove him the prowess and pride of the Geats,
shall bid him battle. Blithe to mead
go he that listeth, when light of dawn
605
this morrow morning o'er men of earth,
ether-robed sun from the south shall beam!"
Joyous then was the Jewel-giver,
hoar-haired, war-brave; help awaited
the Bright-Danes' prince, from Beowulf hearing,
610
folk's good shepherd, such firm resolve.
Then was laughter of liegemen loud resounding
with winsome words. Came Wealhtheow forth,
queen of Hrothgar, heedful of courtesy,
gold-decked, greeting the guests in hall;
615
and the high-born lady handed the cup
first to the East-Danes' heir and warden,
bade him be blithe at the beer-carouse,
the land's beloved one. Lustily took he
banquet and beaker, battle-famed king.
620
Through the hall then went the Helmings' Lady,
to younger and older everywhere
carried the cup, till come the moment
when the ring-graced queen, the royal-hearted,
to Beowulf bore the beaker of mead.
625
She greeted the Geats' lord, God she thanked,
in wisdom's words, that her will was granted,
that at last on a hero her hope could lean

fyrena frofre.   He þæt ful geþeah,
wælreow wiga,   æt Wealhþeon,
630
ond þa gyddode   guþe gefysed;
Beowulf maþelode,   bearn Ecgþeowes:
"Ic þæt hogode,   þa ic on holm gestah,
sæbat gesæt   mid minra secga gedriht,
þæt ic anunga   eowra leoda
635
willan geworhte   oþðe on wæl crunge,
feondgrapum fæst.   Ic gefremman sceal
eorlic ellen,   oþðe endedæg
on þisse meoduhealle   minne gebidan."
ðam wife þa word   wel licodon,
640
gilpcwide Geates;   eode goldhroden
freolicu folccwen   to hire frean sittan.
þa wæs eft swa ær   inne on healle
þryðword sprecen,   ðeod on sælum,
sigefolca sweg,   oþþæt semninga
645
sunu Healfdenes   secean wolde
æfenræste;   wiste þæm ahlæcan
to þæm heahsele   hilde geþinged,
siððan hie sunnan leoht   geseon ne meahton,
oþðe nipende   niht ofer ealle,
650
scaduhelma gesceapu   scriðan cwoman,
wan under wolcnum.   Werod eall aras.
Gegrette þa   guma oþerne,
Hroðgar Beowulf,   ond him hæl abead,
winærnes geweald,   ond þæt word acwæð:
655
"Næfre ic ænegum men   ær alyfde,
siþðan ic hond ond rond   hebban mihte,
ðryþærn Dena   buton þe nu ða.
Hafa nu ond geheald   husa selest,
gemyne mærþo,   mægenellen cyð,
660
waca wið wraþum.   Ne bið þe wilna gad,
gif þu þæt ellenweorc   aldre gedigest."

for comfort in terrors. The cup he took,
hardy-in-war, from Wealhtheow's hand,
630
and answer uttered the eager-for-combat.
Beowulf spake, bairn of Ecgtheow: --
"This was my thought, when my thanes and I
bent to the ocean and entered our boat,
that I would work the will of your people
635
fully, or fighting fall in death,
in fiend's gripe fast. I am firm to do
an earl's brave deed, or end the days
of this life of mine in the mead-hall here."
Well these words to the woman seemed,
640
Beowulf's battle-boast. -- Bright with gold
the stately dame by her spouse sat down.
Again, as erst, began in hall
warriors' wassail and words of power,
the proud-band's revel, till presently
645
the son of Healfdene hastened to seek
rest for the night; he knew there waited
fight for the fiend in that festal hall,
when the sheen of the sun they saw no more,
and dusk of night sank darkling nigh,
650
and shadowy shapes came striding on,
wan under welkin. The warriors rose.
Man to man, he made harangue,
Hrothgar to Beowulf, bade him hail,
let him wield the wine hall: a word he added: --
655
"Never to any man erst I trusted,
since I could heave up hand and shield,
this noble Dane-Hall, till now to thee.
Have now and hold this house unpeered;
remember thy glory; thy might declare;
660
watch for the foe! No wish shall fail thee
if thou bidest the battle with bold-won life."

Ða him Hroþgar gewat   mid his hæleþa gedryht,
eodur Scyldinga,   ut of healle;
wolde wigfruma   Wealhþeo secan,
665
cwen to gebeddan.   Hæfde kyningwuldor
Grendle togeanes,   swa guman gefrungon,
seleweard aseted;   sundornytte beheold
ymb aldor Dena,   eotonweard abead.
Huru Geata leod   georne truwode
670
modgan mægnes,   metodes hyldo.
ða he him of dyde   isernbyrnan,
helm of hafelan,   sealde his hyrsted sweord,
irena cyst,   ombihtþegne,
ond gehealdan het   hildegeatwe.
675
Gespræc þa se goda   gylpworda sum,
Beowulf Geata,   ær he on bed stige:
"No ic me an herewæsmun   hnagran talige,
guþgeweorca,   þonne Grendel hine;
forþan ic hine sweorde   swebban nelle,
680
aldre beneotan,   þeah ic eal mæge.
Nat he þara goda   þæt he me ongean slea,
rand geheawe,   þeah ðe he rof sie
niþgeweorca;   ac wit on niht sculon
secge ofersittan,   gif he gesecean dear
685
wig ofer wæpen,   ond siþðan witig god
on swa hwæþere hond,   halig dryhten,
mærðo deme,   swa him gemet þince."
Hylde hine þa heaþodeor,   hleorbolster onfeng
eorles andwlitan,   ond hine ymb monig
690
snellic særinc   selereste gebeah.
Nænig heora þohte   þæt he þanon scolde
eft eardlufan   æfre gesecean,
folc oþðe freoburh,   þær he afeded wæs;
ac hie hæfdon gefrunen   þæt hie ær to fela micles
695
in þæm winsele   wældeað fornam,

XI. THE WATCH FOR GRENDEL.

THEN Hrothgar went with his hero-train,
defence-of-Scyldings, forth from hall;
fain would the war-lord Wealhtheow seek,
665
couch of his queen. The King-of-Glory
against this Grendel a guard had set,
so heroes heard, a hall-defender,
who warded the monarch and watched for the monster.
In truth, the Geats' prince gladly trusted
670
his mettle, his might, the mercy of God!
Cast off then his corselet of iron,
helmet from head; to his henchman gave, --
choicest of weapons, -- the well-chased sword,
bidding him guard the gear of battle.
675
Spake then his Vaunt the valiant man,
Beowulf Geat, ere the bed be sought: --
"Of force in fight no feebler I count me,
in grim war-deeds, than Grendel deems him.
Not with the sword, then, to sleep of death
680
his life will I give, though it lie in my power.
No skill is his to strike against me,
my shield to hew though he hardy be,
bold in battle; we both, this night,
shall spurn the sword, if he seek me here,
685
unweaponed, for war. Let wisest God,
sacred Lord, on which side soever
doom decree as he deemeth right."
Reclined then the chieftain, and cheek-pillows held
the head of the earl, while all about him
690
seamen hardy on hall-beds sank.
None of them thought that thence their steps
to the folk and fastness that fostered them,
to the land they loved, would lead them back!
Full well they wist that on warriors many
695
battle-death seized, in the banquet-hall,

Denigea leode.   Ac him dryhten forgeaf
wigspeda gewiofu,   Wedera leodum,
frofor ond fultum,   þæt hie feond heora
ðurh anes cræft   ealle ofercomon,
700
selfes mihtum.   Soð is gecyþed
þæt mihtig god   manna cynnes
weold wideferhð.   Com on wanre niht
scriðan sceadugenga.   Sceotend swæfon,
þa þæt hornreced   healdan scoldon,
705
ealle buton anum.   þæt wæs yldum cuþ
þæt hie ne moste,   þa metod nolde,
se scynscaþa   under sceadu bregdan;
ac he wæccende   wraþum on andan
bad bolgenmod   beadwa geþinges.

of Danish clan. But comfort and help,
war-weal weaving, to Weder folk
the Master gave, that, by might of one,
over their enemy all prevailed,
700
by single strength. In sooth 'tis told
that highest God o'er human kind
hath wielded ever! -- Thro' wan night striding,
came the walker-in-shadow. Warriors slept
whose hest was to guard the gabled hall, --
705
all save one. 'Twas widely known
that against God's will the ghostly ravager
him {34} could not hurl to haunts of darkness;
wakeful, ready, with warrior's wrath,
bold he bided the battle's issue.

710
Ða com of more   under misthleoþum
Grendel gongan,   godes yrre bær;
mynte se manscaða   manna cynnes
sumne besyrwan   in sele þam hean.
Wod under wolcnum   to þæs þe he winreced,
715
goldsele gumena,   gearwost wisse,
fættum fahne.   Ne wæs þæt forma sið
þæt he Hroþgares   ham gesohte;
næfre he on aldordagum   ær ne siþðan
heardran hæle,   healðegnas fand.
720
Com þa to recede   rinc siðian,
dreamum bedæled.   Duru sona onarn,
fyrbendum fæst,   syþðan he hire folmum æthran;
onbræd þa bealohydig,   ða he gebolgen wæs,
recedes muþan.   Raþe æfter þon
725
 on fagne flor   feond treddode,
eode yrremod;   him of eagum stod
ligge gelicost   leoht unfæger.
Geseah he in recede   rinca manige,
swefan sibbegedriht   samod ætgædere,
730
magorinca heap.   þa his mod ahlog;
mynte þæt he gedælde,   ærþon dæg cwome,
atol aglæca,   anra gehwylces
lif wið lice,   þa him alumpen wæs
wistfylle wen.   Ne wæs þæt wyrd þa gen
735
þæt he ma moste   manna cynnes
ðicgean ofer þa niht.   þryðswyð beheold
mæg Higelaces,   hu se manscaða
under færgripum   gefaran wolde.
Ne þæt se aglæca   yldan þohte,
740
ac he gefeng hraðe   forman siðe
slæpendne rinc,   slat unwearnum,
bat banlocan,   blod edrum dranc,

XII. GRENDEL'S RAID.

710
THEN from the moorland, by misty crags,
with God's wrath laden, Grendel came.
The monster was minded of mankind now
sundry to seize in the stately house.
Under welkin he walked, till the wine-palace there,
715
gold-hall of men, he gladly discerned,
flashing with fretwork. Not first time, this,
that he the home of Hrothgar sought, --
yet ne'er in his life-day, late or early,
such hardy heroes, such hall-thanes, found!
720
To the house the warrior walked apace,
parted from peace; {35} the portal opended,
though with forged bolts fast, when his fists had struck it,
and baleful he burst in his blatant rage,
the house's mouth. All hastily, then,
725
o'er fair-paved floor the fiend trod on,
ireful he strode; there streamed from his eyes
fearful flashes, like flame to see.

He spied in hall the hero-band,
kin and clansmen clustered asleep,
730
hardy liegemen. Then laughed his heart;
for the monster was minded, ere morn should dawn,
savage, to sever the soul of each,
life from body, since lusty banquet
waited his will! But Wyrd forbade him
735
to seize any more of men on earth
after that evening. Eagerly watched
Hygelac's kinsman his cursed foe,
how he would fare in fell attack.
Not that the monster was minded to pause!
740
Straightway he seized a sleeping warrior
for the first, and tore him fiercely asunder,
the bone-frame bit, drank blood in streams,

synsnædum swealh;   sona hæfde
unlyfigendes   eal gefeormod,
745
fet ond folma.   Forð near ætstop,
nam þa mid handa   higeþihtigne
rinc on ræste,   ræhte ongean
feond mid folme;   he onfeng hraþe
inwitþancum   ond wið earm gesæt.
750
Sona þæt onfunde   fyrena hyrde
þæt he ne mette   middangeardes,
eorþan sceata,   on elran men
mundgripe maran.   He on mode wearð
forht on ferhðe;   no þy ær fram meahte.
755
Hyge wæs him hinfus,   wolde on heolster fleon,
secan deofla gedræg;   ne wæs his drohtoð þær
swylce he on ealderdagum   ær gemette.
Gemunde þa se goda,   mæg Higelaces,
æfenspræce,   uplang astod
760
ond him fæste wiðfeng;   fingras burston.
Eoten wæs utweard;   eorl furþur stop.
Mynte se mæra,   þær he meahte swa,
widre gewindan   ond on weg þanon
fleon on fenhopu;   wiste his fingra geweald
765
on grames grapum.   þæt wæs geocor sið
þæt se hearmscaþa   to Heorute ateah.
Dryhtsele dynede;   Denum eallum wearð,
ceasterbuendum,   cenra gehwylcum,
eorlum ealuscerwen.   Yrre wæron begen,
770
reþe renweardas.   Reced hlynsode.
þa wæs wundor micel   þæt se winsele
wiðhæfde heaþodeorum,   þæt he on hrusan ne feol,
fæger foldbold;   ac he þæs fæste wæs
innan ond utan   irenbendum
775
searoþoncum besmiþod.   þær fram sylle abeag
medubenc monig,   mine gefræge,
golde geregnad,   þær þa graman wunnon.
þæs ne wendon ær   witan Scyldinga

swallowed him piecemeal: swiftly thus
the lifeless corse was clear devoured,
745
e'en feet and hands. Then farther he hied;
for the hardy hero with hand he grasped,
felt for the foe with fiendish claw,
for the hero reclining, -- who clutched it boldly,
prompt to answer, propped on his arm.
750
Soon then saw that shepherd-of-evils
that never he met in this middle-world,
in the ways of earth, another wight
with heavier hand-gripe; at heart he feared,
sorrowed in soul, -- none the sooner escaped!
755
Fain would he flee, his fastness seek,
the den of devils: no doings now
such as oft he had done in days of old!
Then bethought him the hardy Hygelac-thane
of his boast at evening: up he bounded,
760
grasped firm his foe, whose fingers cracked.
The fiend made off, but the earl close followed.
The monster meant -- if he might at all --
to fling himself free, and far away
fly to the fens, -- knew his fingers' power
765
in the gripe of the grim one. Gruesome march
to Heorot this monster of harm had made!
Din filled the room; the Danes were bereft,
castle-dwellers and clansmen all,
earls, of their ale. Angry were both
770
those savage hall-guards: the house resounded.
Wonder it was the wine-hall firm
in the strain of their struggle stood, to earth
the fair house fell not; too fast it was
within and without by its iron bands
775
craftily clamped; though there crashed from sill
many a mead-bench -- men have told me --
gay with gold, where the grim foes wrestled.
So well had weened the wisest Scyldings

þæt hit a mid gemete   manna ænig,
780
betlic ond banfag,   tobrecan meahte,
listum tolucan,   nymþe liges fæþm
swulge on swaþule.   Sweg up astag
niwe geneahhe;   Norðdenum stod
atelic egesa,   anra gehwylcum
785
þara þe of wealle   wop gehyrdon,
gryreleoð galan   godes ondsacan,
sigeleasne sang,   sar wanigean
helle hæfton.   Heold hine fæste
se þe manna wæs   mægene strengest
790
on þæm dæge   þysses lifes.

that not ever at all might any man
780
that bone-decked, brave house break asunder,
crush by craft, -- unless clasp of fire
in smoke engulfed it. -- Again uprose
din redoubled. Danes of the North
with fear and frenzy were filled, each one,
785
who from the wall that wailing heard,
God's foe sounding his grisly song,
cry of the conquered, clamorous pain
from captive of hell. Too closely held him
he who of men in might was strongest
790
in that same day of this our life.

Nolde eorla hleo   ænige þinga
þone cwealmcuman   cwicne forlætan,
ne his lifdagas   leoda ænigum
nytte tealde.   þær genehost brægd
795
eorl Beowulfes   ealde lafe,
wolde freadrihtnes   feorh ealgian,
mæres þeodnes,   ðær hie meahton swa.
Hie þæt ne wiston,   þa hie gewin drugon,
heardhicgende   hildemecgas,
800
ond on healfa gehwone   heawan þohton,
sawle secan,   þone synscaðan
ænig ofer eorþan   irenna cyst,
guðbilla nan,   gretan nolde,
ac he sigewæpnum   forsworen hæfde,
805
ecga gehwylcre.   Scolde his aldorgedal
on ðæm dæge   þysses lifes
earmlic wurðan,   ond se ellorgast
on feonda geweald   feor siðian.
ða þæt onfunde   se þe fela æror
810
modes myrðe   manna cynne,
fyrene gefremede   (he wæs fag wið god),
þæt him se lichoma   læstan nolde,
ac hine se modega   mæg Hygelaces
hæfde be honda;   wæs gehwæþer oðrum
815
lifigende lað.   Licsar gebad
atol æglæca;   him on eaxle wearð
syndolh sweotol,   seonowe onsprungon,
burston banlocan.   Beowulfe wearð
guðhreð gyfeþe;   scolde Grendel þonan
820
feorhseoc fleon   under fenhleoðu,
secean wynleas wic;   wiste þe geornor
þæt his aldres wæs   ende gegongen,
dogera dægrim.   Denum eallum wearð
æfter þam wælræse   willa gelumpen.

XIII. BEOWULF TEARS OFF GRENDEL'S ARM.

NOT in any wise would the earls'-defence {36}
suffer that slaughterous stranger to live,
useless deeming his days and years
to men on earth. Now many an earl
795
of Beowulf brandished blade ancestral,
fain the life of their lord to shield,
their praised prince, if power were theirs;
never they knew, -- as they neared the foe,
hardy-hearted heroes of war,
800
aiming their swords on every side
the accursed to kill, -- no keenest blade,
no farest of falchions fashioned on earth,
could harm or hurt that hideous fiend!
He was safe, by his spells, from sword of battle,
805
from edge of iron. Yet his end and parting
on that same day of this our life
woful should be, and his wandering soul
far off flit to the fiends' domain.
Soon he found, who in former days,
810
harmful in heart and hated of God,
on many a man such murder wrought,
that the frame of his body failed him now.
For him the keen-souled kinsman of Hygelac
held in hand; hateful alive
815
was each to other. The outlaw dire
took mortal hurt; a mighty wound
showed on his shoulder, and sinews cracked,
and the bone-frame burst. To Beowulf now
the glory was given, and Grendel thence
820
death-sick his den in the dark moor sought,
noisome abode: he knew too well
that here was the last of life, an end
of his days on earth. -- To all the Danes
by that bloody battle the boon had come.

825
Hæfde þa gefælsod   se þe ær feorran com,
snotor ond swyðferhð,   sele Hroðgares,
genered wið niðe;   nihtweorce gefeh,
ellenmærþum.   Hæfde Eastdenum
Geatmecga leod   gilp gelæsted,
830
swylce oncyþðe   ealle gebette,
inwidsorge,   þe hie ær drugon
ond for þreanydum   þolian scoldon,
torn unlytel.   þæt wæs tacen sweotol,
syþðan hildedeor   hond alegde,
835
earm ond eaxle   (þær wæs eal geador
Grendles grape)   under geapne hrof.

825
From ravage had rescued the roving stranger
Hrothgar's hall; the hardy and wise one
had purged it anew. His night-work pleased him,
his deed and its honor. To Eastern Danes
had the valiant Geat his vaunt made good,
830
all their sorrow and ills assuaged,
their bale of battle borne so long,
and all the dole they erst endured
pain a-plenty. -- 'Twas proof of this,
when the hardy-in-fight a hand laid down,
835
arm and shoulder, -- all, indeed,
of Grendel's gripe, -- 'neath the gabled roof.

Ða wæs on morgen mine gefræge
ymb þa gifhealle guðrinc monig;
ferdon folctogan feorran ond nean
840
geond widwegas wundor sceawian,
laþes lastas. No his lifgedal
sarlic þuhte secga ænegum
þara þe tirleases trode sceawode,
hu he werigmod on weg þanon,
845
niða ofercumen, on nicera mere
fæge ond geflymed feorhlastas bær.
ðær wæs on blode brim weallende,
atol yða geswing eal gemenged
haton heolfre, heorodreore weol.
850
Deaðfæge deog, siððan dreama leas
in fenfreoðo feorh alegde,
hæþene sawle; þær him hel onfeng.
þanon eft gewiton ealdgesiðas,
swylce geong manig of gomenwaþe
855
fram mere modge mearum ridan,
beornas on blancum. ðær wæs Beowulfes
mærðo mæned; monig oft gecwæð
þætte suð ne norð be sæm tweonum
ofer eormengrund oþer nænig
860
under swegles begong selra nære
rondhæbbendra, rices wyrðra.
Ne hie huru winedrihten wiht ne logon,
glædne Hroðgar, ac þæt wæs god cyning.
Hwilum heaþorofe hleapan leton,
865
on geflit faran fealwe mearas
ðær him foldwegas fægere þuhton,
cystum cuðe. Hwilum cyninges þegn,
guma gilphlæden, gidda gemyndig,
se ðe ealfela ealdgesegena
870
worn gemunde, word oþer fand

XIV. THE JOY AT HEOROT.

MANY at morning, as men have told me,
warriors gathered the gift-hall round,
folk-leaders faring from far and near,
840
o'er wide-stretched ways, the wonder to view,
trace of the traitor. Not troublous seemed
the enemy's end to any man
who saw by the gait of the graceless foe
how the weary-hearted, away from thence,
845
baffled in battle and banned, his steps
death-marked dragged to the devils' mere.
Bloody the billows were boiling there,
turbid the tide of tumbling waves
horribly seething, with sword-blood hot,
850
by that doomed one dyed, who in den of the moor
laid forlorn his life adown,
his heathen soul, and hell received it.
Home then rode the hoary clansmen
from that merry journey, and many a youth,
855
on horses white, the hardy warriors,
back from the mere. Then Beowulf's glory
eager they echoed, and all averred
that from sea to sea, or south or north,
there was no other in earth's domain,
860
under vault of heaven, more valiant found,
of warriors none more worthy to rule!
(On their lord beloved they laid no slight,
gracious Hrothgar: a good king he!)
From time to time, the tried-in-battle
865
their gray steeds set to gallop amain,
and ran a race when the road seemed fair.
From time to time, a thane of the king,
who had made many vaunts, and was mindful of verses,
stored with sagas and songs of old,
870
bound word to word in well-knit rime,

soðe gebunden;   secg eft ongan
sið Beowulfes   snyttrum styrian
ond on sped wrecan   spel gerade,
wordum wrixlan.   Welhwylc gecwæð
875
þæt he fram Sigemundes   secgan hyrde
ellendædum,   uncuþes fela,
Wælsinges gewin,   wide siðas,
þara þe gumena bearn   gearwe ne wiston,
fæhðe ond fyrena,   buton Fitela mid hine,
880
þonne he swulces hwæt   secgan wolde,
eam his nefan,   swa hie a wæron
æt niða gehwam   nydgesteallan;
hæfdon ealfela   eotena cynnes
sweordum gesæged.   Sigemunde gesprong
885
æfter deaðdæge   dom unlytel,
syþðan wiges heard   wyrm acwealde,
hordes hyrde.   He under harne stan,
æþelinges bearn,   ana geneðde
frecne dæde,   ne wæs him Fitela mid.
890
Hwæþre him gesælde   ðæt þæt swurd þurhwod
wrætlicne wyrm,   þæt hit on wealle ætstod,
dryhtlic iren;   draca morðre swealt.
Hæfde aglæca   elne gegongen
þæt he beahhordes   brucan moste
895
selfes dome;   sæbat gehleod,
bær on bearm scipes   beorhte frætwa,
Wælses eafera.   Wyrm hat gemealt.
Se wæs wreccena   wide mærost
ofer werþeode,   wigendra hleo,
900
ellendædum   (he þæs ær onðah),
siððan Heremodes   hild sweðrode,
eafoð ond ellen.   He mid Eotenum wearð
on feonda geweald   forð forlacen,
snude forsended.   Hine sorhwylmas
905
lemede to lange;   he his leodum wearð,
eallum æþellingum   to aldorceare;

welded his lay; this warrior soon
of Beowulf's quest right cleverly sang,
and artfully added an excellent tale,
in well-ranged words, of the warlike deeds
875
he had heard in saga of Sigemund.
Strange the story: he said it all, --
the Waelsing's wanderings wide, his struggles,
which never were told to tribes of men,
the feuds and the frauds, save to Fitela only,
880
when of these doings he deigned to speak,
uncle to nephew; as ever the twain
stood side by side in stress of war,
and multitude of the monster kind
they had felled with their swords. Of Sigemund grew,
885
when he passed from life, no little praise;
for the doughty-in-combat a dragon killed
that herded the hoard: {37} under hoary rock
the atheling dared the deed alone
fearful quest, nor was Fitela there.
890
Yet so it befell, his falchion pierced
that wondrous worm, -- on the wall it struck,
best blade; the dragon died in its blood.
Thus had the dread-one by daring achieved
over the ring-hoard to rule at will,
895
himself to pleasure; a sea-boat he loaded,
and bore on its bosom the beaming gold,
son of Waels; the worm was consumed.
He had of all heroes the highest renown
among races of men, this refuge-of-warriors,
900
for deeds of daring that decked his name
since the hand and heart of Heremod
grew slack in battle. He, swiftly banished
to mingle with monsters at mercy of foes,
to death was betrayed; for torrents of sorrow
905
had lamed him too long; a load of care
to earls and athelings all he proved.

swylce oft bemearn   ærran mælum
swiðferhþes sið   snotor ceorl monig,
se þe him bealwa to   bote gelyfde,
910
þæt þæt ðeodnes bearn   geþeon scolde,
fæderæþelum onfon,   folc gehealdan,
hord ond hleoburh,   hæleþa rice,
Scyldinga.   He þær eallum wearð,
mæg Higelaces,   manna cynne,
915
freondum gefægra;   hine fyren onwod.
Hwilum flitende   fealwe stræte
mearum mæton.   ða wæs morgenleoht
scofen ond scynded.   Eode scealc monig
swiðhicgende   to sele þam hean
920
searowundor seon;   swylce self cyning
of brydbure,   beahhorda weard,
tryddode tirfæst   getrume micle,
cystum gecyþed,   ond his cwen mid him
medostigge mæt   mægþa hose.

Oft indeed, in earlier days,
for the warrior's wayfaring wise men mourned,
who had hoped of him help from harm and bale,
910
and had thought their sovran's son would thrive,
follow his father, his folk protect,
the hoard and the stronghold, heroes' land,
home of Scyldings. -- But here, thanes said,
the kinsman of Hygelac kinder seemed
915
to all: the other {38} was urged to crime!
And afresh to the race, {39} the fallow roads
by swift steeds measured! The morning sun
was climbing higher. Clansmen hastened
to the high-built hall, those hardy-minded,
920
the wonder to witness. Warden of treasure,
crowned with glory, the king himself,
with stately band from the bride-bower strode;
and with him the queen and her crowd of maidens
measured the path to the mead-house fair.

925
Hroðgar maþelode   (he to healle geong,
stod on stapole,   geseah steapne hrof,
golde fahne,   ond Grendles hond):
"ðisse ansyne   alwealdan þanc
lungre gelimpe!   Fela ic laþes gebad,
930
grynna æt Grendle;   a mæg god wyrcan
wunder æfter wundre,   wuldres hyrde.
ðæt wæs ungeara   þæt ic ænigra me
weana ne wende   to widan feore
bote gebidan,   þonne blode fah
935
husa selest   heorodreorig stod,
wea widscofen   witena gehwylcum
ðara þe ne wendon   þæt hie wideferhð
leoda landgeweorc   laþum beweredon
scuccum ond scinnum.   Nu scealc hafað
940
þurh drihtnes miht   dæd gefremede
ðe we ealle   ær ne meahton
snyttrum besyrwan.   Hwæt, þæt secgan mæg
efne swa hwylc mægþa   swa ðone magan cende
æfter gumcynnum,   gyf heo gyt lyfað,
945
þæt hyre ealdmetod   este wære
bearngebyrdo.   Nu ic, Beowulf, þec,
secg betsta,   me for sunu wylle
freogan on ferhþe;   heald forð tela
niwe sibbe.   Ne bið þe nænigra gad
950
worolde wilna,   þe ic geweald hæbbe.
Ful oft ic for læssan   lean teohhode,
hordweorþunge   hnahran rince,
sæmran æt sæcce.   þu þe self hafast
dædum gefremed   þæt þin dom lyfað
955
awa to aldre.   Alwalda þec
gode forgylde,   swa he nu gyt dyde!"
Beowulf maþelode,   bearn Ecþeowes:

XV. HROTHGAR'S GRATULATION.

925
HROTHGAR spake, -- to the hall he went,
stood by the steps, the steep roof saw,
garnished with gold, and Grendel's hand: --
"For the sight I see to the Sovran Ruler
be speedy thanks! A throng of sorrows
930
I have borne from Grendel; but God still works
wonder on wonder, the Warden-of-Glory.
It was but now that I never more
for woes that weighed on me waited help
long as I lived, when, laved in blood,
935
stood sword-gore-stained this stateliest house, --
widespread woe for wise men all,
who had no hope to hinder ever
foes infernal and fiendish sprites
from havoc in hall. This hero now,
940
by the Wielder's might, a work has done
that not all of us erst could ever do
by wile and wisdom. Lo, well can she say
whoso of women this warrior bore
among sons of men, if still she liveth,
945
that the God of the ages was good to her
in the birth of her bairn. Now, Beowulf, thee,
of heroes best, I shall heartily love
as mine own, my son; preserve thou ever
this kinship new: thou shalt never lack
950
wealth of the world that I wield as mine!
Full oft for less have I largess showered,
my precious hoard, on a punier man,
less stout in struggle. Thyself hast now
fulfilled such deeds, that thy fame shall endure
955
through all the ages. As ever he did,
well may the Wielder reward thee still!"
Beowulf spake, bairn of Ecgtheow: --

"We þæt ellenweorc   estum miclum,
feohtan fremedon,   frecne geneðdon
960
eafoð uncuþes.   Uþe ic swiþor
þæt ðu hine selfne   geseon moste,
feond on frætewum   fylwerigne.
Ic hine hrædlice   heardan clammum
on wælbedde   wriþan þohte,
965
þæt he for mundgripe   minum scolde
licgean lifbysig,   butan his lic swice.
Ic hine ne mihte,   þa metod nolde,
ganges getwæman,   no ic him þæs georne ætfealh,
feorhgeniðlan;   wæs to foremihtig
970
feond on feþe.   Hwæþere he his folme forlet
to lifwraþe   last weardian,
earm ond eaxle.   No þær ænige swa þeah
feasceaft guma   frofre gebohte;
no þy leng leofað   laðgeteona,
975
synnum geswenced,   ac hyne sar hafað
mid nydgripe   nearwe befongen,
balwon bendum.   ðær abidan sceal
maga mane fah   miclan domes,
hu him scir metod   scrifan wille."
980
ða wæs swigra secg,   sunu Eclafes,
on gylpspræce   guðgeweorca,
siþðan æþelingas   eorles cræfte
ofer heanne hrof   hand sceawedon,
feondes fingras.   Foran æghwylc wæs,
985
stiðra nægla gehwylc,   style gelicost,
hæþenes handsporu   hilderinces,
egl, unheoru.   æghwylc gecwæð
þæt him heardra nan   hrinan wolde
iren ærgod,   þæt ðæs ahlæcan
990
blodge beadufolme   onberan wolde.

"This work of war most willingly
we have fought, this fight, and fearlessly dared
960
force of the foe. Fain, too, were I
hadst thou but seen himself, what time
the fiend in his trappings tottered to fall!
Swiftly, I thought, in strongest gripe
on his bed of death to bind him down,
965
that he in the hent of this hand of mine
should breathe his last: but he broke away.
Him I might not -- the Maker willed not --
hinder from flight, and firm enough hold
the life-destroyer: too sturdy was he,
970
the ruthless, in running! For rescue, however,
he left behind him his hand in pledge,
arm and shoulder; nor aught of help
could the cursed one thus procure at all.
None the longer liveth he, loathsome fiend,
975
sunk in his sins, but sorrow holds him
tightly grasped in gripe of anguish,
in baleful bonds, where bide he must,
evil outlaw, such awful doom
as the Mighty Maker shall mete him out."
980
More silent seemed the son of Ecglaf {40}
in boastful speech of his battle-deeds,
since athelings all, through the earl's great prowess,
beheld that hand, on the high roof gazing,
foeman's fingers, -- the forepart of each
985
of the sturdy nails to steel was likest, --
heathen's "hand-spear," hostile warrior's
claw uncanny. 'Twas clear, they said,
that him no blade of the brave could touch,
how keen soever, or cut away
990
that battle-hand bloody from baneful foe.

Ða wæs haten hreþe   Heort innanweard
folmum gefrætwod.   Fela þæra wæs,
wera ond wifa,   þe þæt winreced,
gestsele gyredon.   Goldfag scinon
995
web æfter wagum,   wundorsiona fela
secga gehwylcum   þara þe on swylc starað.
Wæs þæt beorhte bold   tobrocen swiðe,
eal inneweard   irenbendum fæst,
heorras tohlidene.   Hrof ana genæs,
1000
ealles ansund,   þe se aglæca,
fyrendædum fag,   on fleam gewand,
aldres orwena.   No þæt yðe byð
to befleonne,   fremme se þe wille,
ac gesecan sceal   sawlberendra,
1005
nyde genydde,   niþða bearna,
grundbuendra   gearwe stowe,
þær his lichoma   legerbedde fæst
swefeþ æfter symle.   þa wæs sæl ond mæl
þæt to healle gang   Healfdenes sunu;
1010
wolde self cyning   symbel þicgan.
Ne gefrægen ic þa mægþe   maran weorode
ymb hyra sincgyfan   sel gebæran.
Bugon þa to bence   blædagande,
fylle gefægon;   fægere geþægon
1015
medoful manig   magas þara
swiðhicgende   on sele þam hean,
Hroðgar ond Hroþulf.   Heorot innan wæs
freondum afylled;   nalles facenstafas
þeodscyldingas   þenden fremedon.
1020
Forgeaf þa Beowulfe   bearn Healfdenes
segen gyldenne   sigores to leane;
hroden hildecumbor,   helm ond byrnan,
mære maðþumsweord   manige gesawon
beforan beorn beran.   Beowulf geþah

XVI. THE BANQUET AND THE GIFTS.

THERE was hurry and hest in Heorot now
for hands to bedeck it, and dense was the throng
of men and women the wine-hall to cleanse,
the guest-room to garnish. Gold-gay shone the hangings
995
that were wove on the wall, and wonders many
to delight each mortal that looks upon them.
Though braced within by iron bands,
that building bright was broken sorely; {41}
rent were its hinges; the roof alone
1000
held safe and sound, when, seared with crime,
the fiendish foe his flight essayed,
of life despairing. -- No light thing that,
the flight for safety, -- essay it who will!
Forced of fate, he shall find his way
1005
to the refuge ready for race of man,
for soul-possessors, and sons of earth;
and there his body on bed of death
shall rest after revel. Arrived was the hour
when to hall proceeded Healfdene's son:
1010
the king himself would sit to banquet.
Ne'er heard I of host in haughtier throng
more graciously gathered round giver-of-rings!
Bowed then to bench those bearers-of-glory,
fain of the feasting. Featly received
1015
many a mead-cup the mighty-in-spirit,
kinsmen who sat in the sumptuous hall,
Hrothgar and Hrothulf. Heorot now
was filled with friends; the folk of Scyldings
ne'er yet had tried the traitor's deed.
1020
To Beowulf gave the bairn of Healfdene
a gold-wove banner, guerdon of triumph,
broidered battle-flag, breastplate and helmet;
and a splendid sword was seen of many
borne to the brave one. Beowulf took

1025
ful on flette;   no he þære feohgyfte
for sceotendum   scamigan ðorfte.
Ne gefrægn ic freondlicor   feower madmas
golde gegyrede   gummanna fela
in ealobence   oðrum gesellan.
1030
Ymb þæs helmes hrof   heafodbeorge
wirum bewunden   walu utan heold,
þæt him fela laf   frecne ne meahton
scurheard sceþðan,   þonne scyldfreca
ongean gramum   gangan scolde.
1035
Heht ða eorla hleo   eahta mearas
fætedhleore   on flet teon,
in under eoderas.   þara anum stod
sadol searwum fah,   since gewurþad;
þæt wæs hildesetl   heahcyninges,
1040
ðonne sweorda gelac   sunu Healfdenes
efnan wolde.   Næfre on ore læg
widcuþes wig,   ðonne walu feollon.
Ond ða Beowulfe   bega gehwæþres
eodor Ingwina   onweald geteah,
1045
wicga ond wæpna,   het hine wel brucan.
Swa manlice   mære þeoden,
hordweard hæleþa,   heaþoræsas geald
mearum ond madmum,   swa hy næfre man lyhð,
se þe secgan wile   soð æfter rihte.

1025
cup in hall: {42} for such costly gifts
he suffered no shame in that soldier throng.
For I heard of few heroes, in heartier mood,
with four such gifts, so fashioned with gold,
on the ale-bench honoring others thus!
1030
O'er the roof of the helmet high, a ridge,
wound with wires, kept ward o'er the head,
lest the relict-of-files {43} should fierce invade,
sharp in the strife, when that shielded hero
should go to grapple against his foes.
1035
Then the earls'-defence {44} on the floor {45} bade lead
coursers eight, with carven head-gear,
adown the hall: one horse was decked
with a saddle all shining and set in jewels;
'twas the battle-seat of the best of kings,
1040
when to play of swords the son of Healfdene
was fain to fare. Ne'er failed his valor
in the crush of combat when corpses fell.
To Beowulf over them both then gave
the refuge-of-Ingwines right and power,
1045
o'er war-steeds and weapons: wished him joy of them.
Manfully thus the mighty prince,
hoard-guard for heroes, that hard fight repaid
with steeds and treasures contemned by none
who is willing to say the sooth aright.

1050
Ða gyt æghwylcum   eorla drihten
þara þe mid Beowulfe   brimlade teah
on þære medubence   maþðum gesealde,
yrfelafe,   ond þone ænne heht
golde forgyldan,   þone ðe Grendel ær
1055
mane acwealde,   swa he hyra ma wolde,
nefne him witig god   wyrd forstode
ond ðæs mannes mod.   Metod eallum weold
gumena cynnes,   swa he nu git deð.
Forþan bið andgit   æghwær selest,
1060
ferhðes foreþanc.   Fela sceal gebidan
leofes ond laþes   se þe longe her
on ðyssum windagum   worolde bruceð.
þær wæs sang ond sweg   samod ætgædere
fore Healfdenes   hildewisan,
1065
gomenwudu greted,   gid oft wrecen,
ðonne healgamen   Hroþgares scop
æfter medobence   mænan scolde
be Finnes eaferum,   ða hie se fær begeat,
hæleð Healfdena,   Hnæf Scyldinga,
1070
in Freswæle   feallan scolde.
Ne huru Hildeburh   herian þorfte
Eotena treowe;   unsynnum wearð
beloren leofum   æt þam lindplegan,
bearnum ond broðrum;   hie on gebyrd hruron,
1075
gare wunde.   þæt wæs geomuru ides!
Nalles holinga   Hoces dohtor
meotodsceaft bemearn,   syþðan morgen com,
ða heo under swegle   geseon meahte
morþorbealo maga,   þær heo ær mæste heold
1080
worolde wynne.   Wig ealle fornam
Finnes þegnas   nemne feaum anum,
þæt he ne mehte   on þæm meðelstede

XVII. SONG OF HROTHGAR'S POET.
-THE LAY OF HNAEF AND HENGEST.

1050
AND the lord of earls, to each that came
with Beowulf over the briny ways,
an heirloom there at the ale-bench gave,
precious gift; and the price {46} bade pay
in gold for him whom Grendel erst
1055
murdered, -- and fain of them more had killed,
had not wisest God their Wyrd averted,
and the man's {47} brave mood. The Maker then
ruled human kind, as here and now.
Therefore is insight always best,
1060
and forethought of mind. How much awaits him
of lief and of loath, who long time here,
through days of warfare this world endures!
Then song and music mingled sounds
in the presence of Healfdene's head-of-armies {48}
1065
and harping was heard with the hero-lay
as Hrothgar's singer the hall-joy woke
along the mead-seats, making his song
of that sudden raid on the sons of Finn. {49}
Healfdene's hero, Hnaef the Scylding,
1070
was fated to fall in the Frisian slaughter. {50}
Hildeburh needed not hold in value
her enemies' honor! {51} Innocent both
were the loved ones she lost at the linden-play,
bairn and brother, they bowed to fate,
1075
stricken by spears; 'twas a sorrowful woman!
None doubted why the daughter of Hoc
bewailed her doom when dawning came,
and under the sky she saw them lying,
kinsmen murdered, where most she had kenned
1080
of the sweets of the world! By war were swept, too,
Finn's own liegemen, and few were left;
in the parleying-place {52} he could ply no longer

wig Hengeste   wiht gefeohtan,
ne þa wealafe   wige forþringan
1085
þeodnes ðegna;   ac hig him geþingo budon,
þæt hie him oðer flet   eal gerymdon,
healle ond heahsetl,   þæt hie healfre geweald
wið Eotena bearn   agan moston,
ond æt feohgyftum   Folcwaldan sunu
1090
dogra gehwylce   Dene weorþode,
Hengestes heap   hringum wenede
efne swa swiðe   sincgestreonum
fættan goldes,   swa he Fresena cyn
on beorsele   byldan wolde.
1095
ða hie getruwedon   on twa healfa
fæste frioðuwære.   Fin Hengeste
elne, unflitme   aðum benemde
þæt he þa wealafe   weotena dome
arum heolde,   þæt ðær ænig mon
1100
wordum ne worcum   wære ne bræce,
ne þurh inwitsearo   æfre gemænden
ðeah hie hira beaggyfan   banan folgedon
ðeodenlease,   þa him swa geþearfod wæs;
gyf þonne Frysna hwylc   frecnan spræce
1105
ðæs morþorhetes   myndgiend wære,
þonne hit sweordes ecg   seðan scolde.
Ad wæs geæfned   ond icge gold
ahæfen of horde.   Herescyldinga
betst beadorinca   wæs on bæl gearu.
1110
æt þæm ade wæs   eþgesyne
swatfah syrce,   swyn ealgylden,
eofer irenheard,   æþeling manig
wundum awyrded;   sume on wæle crungon.
Het ða Hildeburh   æt Hnæfes ade
1115
hire selfre sunu   sweoloðe befæstan,
banfatu bærnan   ond on bæl don
eame on eaxle.   Ides gnornode,
geomrode giddum.   Guðrinc astah.

weapon, nor war could he wage on Hengest,
and rescue his remnant by right of arms
1085
from the prince's thane. A pact he offered:
another dwelling the Danes should have,
hall and high-seat, and half the power
should fall to them in Frisian land;
and at the fee-gifts, Folcwald's son
1090
day by day the Danes should honor,
the folk of Hengest favor with rings,
even as truly, with treasure and jewels,
with fretted gold, as his Frisian kin
he meant to honor in ale-hall there.
1095
Pact of peace they plighted further
on both sides firmly. Finn to Hengest
with oath, upon honor, openly promised
that woful remnant, with wise-men's aid,
nobly to govern, so none of the guests
1100
by word or work should warp the treaty, {53}
or with malice of mind bemoan themselves
as forced to follow their fee-giver's slayer,
lordless men, as their lot ordained.
Should Frisian, moreover, with foeman's taunt,
1105
that murderous hatred to mind recall,
then edge of the sword must seal his doom.
Oaths were given, and ancient gold
heaped from hoard. -- The hardy Scylding,
battle-thane best, {54} on his balefire lay.
1110
All on the pyre were plain to see
the gory sark, the gilded swine-crest,
boar of hard iron, and athelings many
slain by the sword: at the slaughter they fell.
It was Hildeburh's hest, at Hnaef's own pyre
1115
the bairn of her body on brands to lay,
his bones to burn, on the balefire placed,
at his uncle's side. In sorrowful dirges
bewept them the woman: great wailing ascended.

Wand to wolcnum   wælfyra mæst,
1120
hlynode for hlawe;   hafelan multon,
bengeato burston,   ðonne blod ætspranc,
laðbite lices.   Lig ealle forswealg,
gæsta gifrost,   þara ðe þær guð fornam
bega folces;   wæs hira blæd scacen.

Then wound up to welkin the wildest of death-fires,
1120
roared o'er the hillock: {55} heads all were melted,
gashes burst, and blood gushed out
from bites {56} of the body. Balefire devoured,
greediest spirit, those spared not by war
out of either folk: their flower was gone.

1125
Gewiton him ða wigend   wica neosian,
freondum befeallen,   Frysland geseon,
hamas ond heaburh.   Hengest ða gyt
wælfagne winter   wunode mid Finne
eal unhlitme.   Eard gemunde,
1130
þeah þe he ne meahte   on mere drifan
hringedstefnan;   holm storme weol,
won wið winde,   winter yþe beleac
isgebinde,   oþðæt oþer com
gear in geardas,   swa nu gyt deð,
1135
þa ðe syngales   sele bewitiað,
wuldortorhtan weder.   ða wæs winter scacen,
fæger foldan bearm.   Fundode wrecca,
gist of geardum;   he to gyrnwræce
swiðor þohte   þonne to sælade,
1140
gif he torngemot   þurhteon mihte
þæt he Eotena bearn   inne gemunde.
Swa he ne forwyrnde   woroldrædenne,
þonne him Hunlafing   hildeleoman,
billa selest,   on bearm dyde,
1145
þæs wæron mid Eotenum   ecge cuðe.
Swylce ferhðfrecan   Fin eft begeat
sweordbealo sliðen   æt his selfes ham,
siþðan grimne gripe   Guðlaf ond Oslaf
æfter sæsiðe,   sorge, mændon,
1150
ætwiton weana dæl;   ne meahte wæfre mod
forhabban in hreþre.   ða wæs heal roden
feonda feorum,   swilce Fin slægen,
cyning on corþre,   ond seo cwen numen.
Sceotend Scyldinga   to scypon feredon
1155
eal ingesteald   eorðcyninges,
swylce hie æt Finnes ham   findan meahton
sigla, searogimma.   Hie on sælade
drihtlice wif   to Denum feredon,

XVIII. THE GLEEMAN'S TALE IS ENDED.

1125
THEN hastened those heroes their home to see,
friendless, to find the Frisian land,
houses and high burg. Hengest still
through the death-dyed winter dwelt with Finn,
holding pact, yet of home he minded,
1130
though powerless his ring-decked prow to drive
over the waters, now waves rolled fierce
lashed by the winds, or winter locked them
in icy fetters. Then fared another
year to men's dwellings, as yet they do,
1135
the sunbright skies, that their season ever
duly await. Far off winter was driven;
fair lay earth's breast; and fain was the rover,
the guest, to depart, though more gladly he pondered
on wreaking his vengeance than roaming the deep,
1140
and how to hasten the hot encounter
where sons of the Frisians were sure to be.
So he escaped not the common doom,
when Hun with "Lafing," the light-of-battle,
best of blades, his bosom pierced:
1145
its edge was famed with the Frisian earls.
On fierce-heart Finn there fell likewise,
on himself at home, the horrid sword-death;
for Guthlaf and Oslaf of grim attack
had sorrowing told, from sea-ways landed,
1150
mourning their woes. {57} Finn's wavering spirit
bode not in breast. The burg was reddened
with blood of foemen, and Finn was slain,
king amid clansmen; the queen was taken.
To their ship the Scylding warriors bore
1155
all the chattels the chieftain owned,
whatever they found in Finn's domain
of gems and jewels. The gentle wife
o'er paths of the deep to the Danes they bore,

læddon to leodum.   Leoð wæs asungen,
1160
gleomannes gyd.   Gamen eft astah,
beorhtode bencsweg;   byrelas sealdon
win of wunderfatum.   þa cwom Wealhþeo forð
gan under gyldnum beage,   þær þa godan twegen
sæton suhtergefæderan;   þa gyt wæs hiera sib
ætgædere,
1165
æghwylc oðrum trywe.   Swylce þær Unferþ þyle
æt fotum sæt frean Scyldinga;   gehwylc hiora his
ferhþe treowde,
þæt he hæfde mod micel,   þeah þe he his magum
nære
arfæst æt ecga gelacum.   Spræc ða ides Scyldinga:
"Onfoh þissum fulle,   freodrihten min,
1170
sinces brytta!   þu on sælum wes,
goldwine gumena,   ond to Geatum spræc
mildum wordum,   swa sceal man don.
Beo wið Geatas glæd,   geofena gemyndig,
nean ond feorran   þu nu hafast.
1175
Me man sægde   þæt þu ðe for sunu wolde
hererinc habban.   Heorot is gefælsod,
beahsele beorhta;   bruc þenden þu mote
manigra medo,   ond þinum magum læf
folc ond rice,   þonne ðu forð scyle
1180
metodsceaft seon.   Ic minne can
glædne Hroþulf,   þæt he þa geogoðe wile
arum healdan,   gyf þu ær þonne he,
wine Scildinga,   worold oflætest;
wene ic þæt he mid gode   gyldan wille
1185
uncran eaferan,   gif he þæt eal gemon,
hwæt wit to willan   ond to worðmyndum
umborwesendum ær   arna gefremedon."
Hwearf þa bi bence   þær hyre byre wæron,
Hreðric ond Hroðmund,   ond hæleþa bearn,
1190
giogoð ætgædere;   þær se goda sæt,
1160

led to her land. The lay was finished,
1160
the gleeman's song. Then glad rose the revel;
bench-joy brightened. Bearers draw
from their "wonder-vats" wine. Comes Wealhtheow forth,
under gold-crown goes where the good pair sit,
uncle and nephew, true each to the other one,
1165
kindred in amity. Unferth the spokesman
at the Scylding lord's feet sat: men had faith in his spirit,
his keenness of courage, though kinsmen had found him
unsure at the sword-play. The Scylding queen spoke:
"Quaff of this cup, my king and lord,
1170
breaker of rings, and blithe be thou,
gold-friend of men; to the Geats here speak
such words of mildness as man should use.
Be glad with thy Geats; of those gifts be mindful,
or near or far, which now thou hast.
1175
Men say to me, as son thou wishest
yon hero to hold. Thy Heorot purged,
jewel-hall brightest, enjoy while thou canst,
with many a largess; and leave to thy kin
folk and realm when forth thou goest
1180
to greet thy doom. For gracious I deem
my Hrothulf, {58} willing to hold and rule
nobly our youths, if thou yield up first,
prince of Scyldings, thy part in the world.
I ween with good he will well requite
1185
offspring of ours, when all he minds
that for him we did in his helpless days
of gift and grace to gain him honor!"
Then she turned to the seat where her sons were placed,
Hrethric and Hrothmund, with heroes' bairns,
1190
young men together: the Geat, too, sat there,
Beowulf brave, the brothers between.

Beowulf Geata,   be þæm gebroðrum twæm.
Him wæs ful boren   ond freondlaþu
wordum bewægned,   ond wunden gold
estum geeawed,   earmreade twa,
1195
hrægl ond hringas,   healsbeaga mæst
þara þe ic on foldan   gefrægen hæbbe.
Nænigne ic under swegle   selran hyrde
hordmaððum hæleþa,   syþðan Hama ætwæg
to þære byrhtan byrig   Brosinga mene,
1200
sigle ond sincfæt;   searoniðas fleah
Eormenrices,   geceas ecne ræd.
þone hring hæfde   Higelac Geata,
nefa Swertinges,   nyhstan siðe,
siðþan he under segne   sinc ealgode,
1205
wælreaf werede;   hyne wyrd fornam,
syþðan he for wlenco   wean ahsode,
fæhðe to Frysum.   He þa frætwe wæg,
eorclanstanas   ofer yða ful,
rice þeoden;   he under rande gecranc.
1210
Gehwearf þa in Francna fæþm   feorh cyninges,
breostgewædu   ond se beah somod;
wyrsan wigfrecan   wæl reafedon
æfter guðsceare,   Geata leode,
hreawic heoldon.   Heal swege onfeng.
1215
Wealhðeo maþelode,   heo fore þæm werede spræc:
"Bruc ðisses beages,   Beowulf leofa,
hyse, mid hæle,   ond þisses hrægles neot,
þeodgestreona,   ond geþeoh tela,
cen þec mid cræfte   ond þyssum cnyhtum wes
1220
lara liðe;   ic þe þæs lean geman.
Hafast þu gefered   þæt ðe feor ond neah
ealne wideferhþ   weras ehtigað,
efne swa side   swa sæ bebugeð,
windgeard, weallas.   Wes þenden þu lifige,

XIX. BEOWULF'S JEWELLED COLLAR.
-THE HEROES REST.

A CUP she gave him, with kindly greeting
and winsome words. Of wounden gold,
she offered, to honor him, arm-jewels twain,
1195
corselet and rings, and of collars the noblest
that ever I knew the earth around.
Ne'er heard I so mighty, 'neath heaven's dome,
a hoard-gem of heroes, since Hama bore
to his bright-built burg the Brisings' necklace,
1200
jewel and gem casket. -- Jealousy fled he,
Eormenric's hate: chose help eternal.
Hygelac Geat, grandson of Swerting,
on the last of his raids this ring bore with him,
under his banner the booty defending,
1205
the war-spoil warding; but Wyrd o'erwhelmed him
what time, in his daring, dangers he sought,
feud with Frisians. Fairest of gems
he bore with him over the beaker-of-waves,
sovran strong: under shield he died.
1210
Fell the corpse of the king into keeping of Franks,
gear of the breast, and that gorgeous ring;
weaker warriors won the spoil,
after gripe of battle, from Geatland's lord,
and held the death-field. Din rose in hall.
1215
Wealhtheow spake amid warriors, and said: --
"This jewel enjoy in thy jocund youth,
Beowulf lov'd, these battle-weeds wear,
a royal treasure, and richly thrive!
Preserve thy strength, and these striplings here
1220
counsel in kindness: requital be mine.
Hast done such deeds, that for days to come
thou art famed among folk both far and near,
so wide as washeth the wave of Ocean
his windy walls. Through the ways of life

1225
æþeling, eadig. Ic þe an tela
sincgestreona. Beo þu suna minum
dædum gedefe, dreamhealdende.
Her is æghwylc eorl oþrum getrywe,
modes milde, mandrihtne hold;
1230
þegnas syndon geþwære, þeod ealgearo,
druncne dryhtguman doð swa ic bidde."
Eode þa to setle. þær wæs symbla cyst;
druncon win weras. Wyrd ne cuþon,
geosceaft grimme, swa hit agangen wearð
1235
eorla manegum, syþðan æfen cwom
ond him Hroþgar gewat to hofe sinum,
rice to ræste. Reced weardode
unrim eorla, swa hie oft ær dydon.
Bencþelu beredon; hit geondbræded wearð
1240
beddum ond bolstrum. Beorscealca sum
fus ond fæge fletræste gebeag.
Setton him to heafdon hilderandas,
bordwudu beorhtan; þær on bence wæs
ofer æþelinge yþgesene
1245
heaþosteapa helm, hringed byrne,
þrecwudu þrymlic. Wæs þeaw hyra
þæt hie oft wæron an wig gearwe,
ge æt ham ge on herge, ge gehwæþer þara,
efne swylce mæla swylce hira mandryhtne
1250
þearf gesælde; wæs seo þeod tilu.

1225
prosper, O prince! I pray for thee
rich possessions. To son of mine
be helpful in deed and uphold his joys!
Here every earl to the other is true,
mild of mood, to the master loyal!
1230
Thanes are friendly, the throng obedient,
liegemen are revelling: list and obey!"
Went then to her place. -- That was proudest of feasts;
flowed wine for the warriors. Wyrd they knew not,
destiny dire, and the doom to be seen
1235
by many an earl when eve should come,
and Hrothgar homeward hasten away,
royal, to rest. The room was guarded
by an army of earls, as erst was done.
They bared the bench-boards; abroad they spread
1240
beds and bolsters. -- One beer-carouser
in danger of doom lay down in the hall. --
At their heads they set their shields of war,
bucklers bright; on the bench were there
over each atheling, easy to see,
1245
the high battle-helmet, the haughty spear,
the corselet of rings. 'Twas their custom so
ever to be for battle prepared,
at home, or harrying, which it were,
even as oft as evil threatened
1250
their sovran king. -- They were clansmen good.

Sigon þa to slæpe.   Sum sare angeald
æfenræste,   swa him ful oft gelamp,
siþðan goldsele   Grendel warode,
unriht æfnde,   oþþæt ende becwom,
1255
swylt æfter synnum.   þæt gesyne wearþ,
widcuþ werum,   þætte wrecend þa gyt
lifde æfter laþum,   lange þrage,
æfter guðceare.   Grendles modor,
ides, aglæcwif,   yrmþe gemunde,
1260
se þe wæteregesan   wunian scolde,
cealde streamas,   siþðan Cain wearð
to ecgbanan   angan breþer,
fæderenmæge;   he þa fag gewat,
morþre gemearcod,   mandream fleon,
1265
westen warode.   þanon woc fela
geosceaftgasta;   wæs þæra Grendel sum,
heorowearh hetelic,   se æt Heorote fand
wæccendne wer   wiges bidan.
þær him aglæca   ætgræpe wearð;
1270
hwæþre he gemunde   mægenes strenge,
gimfæste gife   ðe him god sealde,
ond him to anwaldan   are gelyfde,
frofre ond fultum;   ðy he þone feond ofercwom,
gehnægde helle gast.   þa he hean gewat,
1275
dreame bedæled,   deaþwic seon,
mancynnes feond,   ond his modor þa gyt,
gifre ond galgmod,   gegan wolde
sorhfulne sið,   sunu deað wrecan.
Com þa to Heorote,   ðær Hringdene
1280
geond þæt sæld swæfun.   þa ðær sona wearð
edhwyrft eorlum,   siþðan inne fealh
Grendles modor.   Wæs se gryre læssa
efne swa micle   swa bið mægþa cræft,
wiggryre wifes,   be wæpnedmen,
1285

XX. GRENDEL'S MOTHER ATTACKS THE RING DANES.

THEN sank they to sleep. With sorrow one bought
his rest of the evening, -- as ofttime had happened
when Grendel guarded that golden hall,
evil wrought, till his end drew nigh,
1255
slaughter for sins. 'Twas seen and told
how an avenger survived the fiend,
as was learned afar. The livelong time
after that grim fight, Grendel's mother,
monster of women, mourned her woe.
1260
She was doomed to dwell in the dreary waters,
cold sea-courses, since Cain cut down
with edge of the sword his only brother,
his father's offspring: outlawed he fled,
marked with murder, from men's delights
1265
warded the wilds. -- There woke from him
such fate-sent ghosts as Grendel, who,
war-wolf horrid, at Heorot found
a warrior watching and waiting the fray,
with whom the grisly one grappled amain.
1270
But the man remembered his mighty power,
the glorious gift that God had sent him,
in his Maker's mercy put his trust
for comfort and help: so he conquered the foe,
felled the fiend, who fled abject,
1275
reft of joy, to the realms of death,
mankind's foe. And his mother now,
gloomy and grim, would go that quest
of sorrow, the death of her son to avenge.
To Heorot came she, where helmeted Danes
1280
slept in the hall. Too soon came back
old ills of the earls, when in she burst,
the mother of Grendel. Less grim, though, that terror,
e'en as terror of woman in war is less,
might of maid, than of men in arms
1285

þonne heoru bunden, hamere geþuren,
sweord swate fah swin ofer helme
ecgum dyhttig andweard scireð.
þa wæs on healle heardecg togen
sweord ofer setlum, sidrand manig
1290
hafen handa fæst; helm ne gemunde,
byrnan side, þa hine se broga angeat.
Heo wæs on ofste, wolde ut þanon,
feore beorgan, þa heo onfunden wæs.
Hraðe heo æþelinga anne hæfde
1295
fæste befangen, þa heo to fenne gang.
Se wæs Hroþgare hæleþa leofost
on gesiðes had be sæm tweonum,
rice randwiga, þone ðe heo on ræste abreat,
blædfæstne beorn. Næs Beowulf ðær,
1300
ac wæs oþer in ær geteohhod
æfter maþðumgife mærum Geate.
Hream wearð in Heorote; heo under heolfre genam
cuþe folme; cearu wæs geniwod,
geworden in wicun. Ne wæs þæt gewrixle til,
1305
þæt hie on ba healfa bicgan scoldon
freonda feorum. þa wæs frod cyning,
har hilderinc, on hreon mode,
syðþan he aldorþegn unlyfigendne,
þone deorestan deadne wisse.
1310
Hraþe wæs to bure Beowulf fetod,
sigoreadig secg. Samod ærdæge
eode eorla sum, æþele cempa
self mid gesiðum þær se snotera bad,
hwæþer him alwalda æfre wille
1315
æfter weaspelle wyrpe gefremman.
Gang ða æfter flore fyrdwyrðe man
mid his handscale (healwudu dynede),
þæt he þone wisan wordum nægde
frean Ingwina, frægn gif him wære
1320
æfter neodlaðum niht getæse.

when, hammer-forged, the falchion hard,
sword gore-stained, through swine of the helm,
crested, with keen blade carves amain.
Then was in hall the hard-edge drawn,
the swords on the settles, {59} and shields a-many
1290
firm held in hand: nor helmet minded
nor harness of mail, whom that horror seized.
Haste was hers; she would hie afar
and save her life when the liegemen saw her.
Yet a single atheling up she seized
1295
fast and firm, as she fled to the moor.
He was for Hrothgar of heroes the dearest,
of trusty vassals betwixt the seas,
whom she killed on his couch, a clansman famous,
in battle brave. -- Nor was Beowulf there;
1300
another house had been held apart,
after giving of gold, for the Geat renowned. --
Uproar filled Heorot; the hand all had viewed,
blood-flecked, she bore with her; bale was returned,
dole in the dwellings: 'twas dire exchange
1305
where Dane and Geat were doomed to give
the lives of loved ones. Long-tried king,
the hoary hero, at heart was sad
when he knew his noble no more lived,
and dead indeed was his dearest thane.
1310
To his bower was Beowulf brought in haste,
dauntless victor. As daylight broke,
along with his earls the atheling lord,
with his clansmen, came where the king abode
waiting to see if the Wielder-of-All
1315
would turn this tale of trouble and woe.
Strode o'er floor the famed-in-strife,
with his hand-companions, -- the hall resounded, --
wishing to greet the wise old king,
Ingwines' lord; he asked if the night
1320
had passed in peace to the prince's mind.

Hroðgar maþelode,   helm Scyldinga:
"Ne frin þu æfter sælum!   Sorh is geniwod
Denigea leodum.   Dead is æschere,
Yrmenlafes   yldra broþor,
1325
min runwita   ond min rædbora,
eaxlgestealla,   ðonne we on orlege
hafelan weredon,   þonne hniton feþan,
eoferas cnysedan.   Swylc scolde eorl wesan,
æþeling ærgod,   swylc æschere wæs!
1330
Wearð him on Heorote   to handbanan
wælgæst wæfre;   ic ne wat hwæder
atol æse wlanc   eftsiðas teah,
fylle gefægnod.   Heo þa fæhðe wræc
þe þu gystran niht   Grendel cwealdest
1335
þurh hæstne had   heardum clammum,
forþan he to lange   leode mine
wanode ond wyrde.   He æt wige gecrang
ealdres scyldig,   ond nu oþer cwom
mihtig manscaða,   wolde hyre mæg wrecan,
1340
ge feor hafað   fæhðe gestæled
(þæs þe þincean mæg   þegne monegum,
se þe æfter sincgyfan   on sefan greoteþ),
hreþerbealo hearde;   nu seo hand ligeð,
se þe eow welhwylcra   wilna dohte.
1345
Ic þæt londbuend,   leode mine,
selerædende,   secgan hyrde
þæt hie gesawon   swylce twegen
micle mearcstapan   moras healdan,
ellorgæstas.   ðæra oðer wæs,
1350
þæs þe hie gewislicost   gewitan meahton,
idese onlicnæs;   oðer earmsceapen
on weres wæstmum   wræclastas træd,
næfne he wæs mara   þonne ænig man oðer;
þone on geardagum   Grendel nemdon

XXI. SORROW AT HEOROT.
- AESCHERE'S DEATH.

HROTHGAR spake, helmet-of-Scyldings: --
"Ask not of pleasure! Pain is renewed
to Danish folk. Dead is Aeschere,
of Yrmenlaf the elder brother,
1325
my sage adviser and stay in council,
shoulder-comrade in stress of fight
when warriors clashed and we warded our heads,
hewed the helm-boars; hero famed
should be every earl as Aeschere was!
1330
But here in Heorot a hand hath slain him
of wandering death-sprite. I wot not whither, {60}
proud of the prey, her path she took,
fain of her fill. The feud she avenged
that yesternight, unyieldingly,
1335
Grendel in grimmest grasp thou killedst, --
seeing how long these liegemen mine
he ruined and ravaged. Reft of life,
in arms he fell. Now another comes,
keen and cruel, her kin to avenge,
1340
faring far in feud of blood:
so that many a thane shall think, who e'er
sorrows in soul for that sharer of rings,
this is hardest of heart-bales. The hand lies low
that once was willing each wish to please.
1345
Land-dwellers here {61} and liegemen mine,
who house by those parts, I have heard relate
that such a pair they have sometimes seen,
march-stalkers mighty the moorland haunting,
wandering spirits: one of them seemed,
1350
so far as my folk could fairly judge,
of womankind; and one, accursed,
in man's guise trod the misery-track
of exile, though huger than human bulk.
Grendel in days long gone they named him,

1355
foldbuende.   No hie fæder cunnon,
hwæþer him ænig wæs   ær acenned
dyrnra gasta.   Hie dygel lond
warigeað, wulfhleoþu,   windige næssas,
frecne fengelad,   ðær fyrgenstream
1360
under næssa genipu   niþer gewiteð,
flod under foldan.   Nis þæt feor heonon
milgemearces   þæt se mere standeð;
ofer þæm hongiað   hrinde bearwas,
wudu wyrtum fæst   wæter oferhelmað.
1365
þær mæg nihta gehwæm   niðwundor seon,
fyr on flode.   No þæs frod leofað
gumena bearna,   þæt þone grund wite;
ðeah þe hæðstapa   hundum geswenced,
heorot hornum trum,   holtwudu sece,
1370
feorran geflymed,   ær he feorh seleð,
aldor on ofre,   ær he in wille
hafelan hydan.   Nis þæt heoru stow!
þonon yðgeblond   up astigeð
won to wolcnum,   þonne wind styreþ,
1375
lað gewidru,   oðþæt lyft drysmaþ,
roderas reotað.   Nu is se ræd gelang
eft æt þe anum.   Eard git ne const,
frecne stowe,   ðær þu findan miht
felasinnigne secg;   sec gif þu dyrre.
1380
Ic þe þa fæhðe   feo leanige,
ealdgestreonum,   swa ic ær dyde,
wundnum golde,   gyf þu on weg cymest."

1355
folk of the land; his father they knew not,
nor any brood that was born to him
of treacherous spirits. Untrod is their home;
by wolf-cliffs haunt they and windy headlands,
fenways fearful, where flows the stream
1360
from mountains gliding to gloom of the rocks,
underground flood. Not far is it hence
in measure of miles that the mere expands,
and o'er it the frost-bound forest hanging,
sturdily rooted, shadows the wave.
1365
By night is a wonder weird to see,
fire on the waters. So wise lived none
of the sons of men, to search those depths!
Nay, though the heath-rover, harried by dogs,
the horn-proud hart, this holt should seek,
1370
long distance driven, his dear life first
on the brink he yields ere he brave the plunge
to hide his head: 'tis no happy place!
Thence the welter of waters washes up
wan to welkin when winds bestir
1375
evil storms, and air grows dusk,
and the heavens weep. Now is help once more
with thee alone! The land thou knowst not,
place of fear, where thou findest out
that sin-flecked being. Seek if thou dare!
1380
I will reward thee, for waging this fight,
with ancient treasure, as erst I did,
with winding gold, if thou winnest back."

Beowulf maþelode,   bearn Ecgþeowes:
"Ne sorga, snotor guma;   selre bið æghwæm
1385
þæt he his freond wrece,   þonne he fela murne.
Ure æghwylc sceal   ende gebidan
worolde lifes;   wyrce se þe mote
domes ær deaþe;   þæt bið drihtguman
unlifgendum   æfter selest.
1390
Aris, rices weard,   uton raþe feran
Grendles magan   gang sceawigan.
Ic hit þe gehate,   no he on helm losaþ,
ne on foldan fæþm,   ne on fyrgenholt,
ne on gyfenes grund,   ga þær he wille.
1395
ðys dogor þu   geþyld hafa
weana gehwylces,   swa ic þe wene to."
Ahleop ða se gomela,   gode þancode,
mihtigan drihtne,   þæs se man gespræc.
þa wæs Hroðgare   hors gebæted,
1400
wicg wundenfeax.   Wisa fengel
geatolic gende;   gumfeþa stop
lindhæbbendra.   Lastas wæron
æfter waldswaþum   wide gesyne,
gang ofer grundas,   þær heo gegnum for
1405
ofer myrcan mor,   magoþegna bær
þone selestan   sawolleasne
þara þe mid Hroðgare   ham eahtode.
Ofereode þa   æþelinga bearn
steap stanhliðo,   stige nearwe,
1410
enge anpaðas,   uncuð gelad,
neowle næssas,   nicorhusa fela.
He feara sum   beforan gengde
wisra monna   wong sceawian,
oþþæt he færinga   fyrgenbeamas
1415
ofer harne stan   hleonian funde,

XXII. BEOWULF SEEKS THE MONSTER IN THE HAUNTS OF THE NIXIES.

BEOWULF spake, bairn of Ecgtheow:
"Sorrow not, sage! It beseems us better
1385
friends to avenge than fruitlessly mourn them.
Each of us all must his end abide
in the ways of the world; so win who may
glory ere death! When his days are told,
that is the warrior's worthiest doom.
1390
Rise, O realm-warder! Ride we anon,
and mark the trail of the mother of Grendel.
No harbor shall hide her -- heed my promise! --
enfolding of field or forested mountain
or floor of the flood, let her flee where she will!
1395
But thou this day endure in patience,
as I ween thou wilt, thy woes each one."
Leaped up the graybeard: God he thanked,
mighty Lord, for the man's brave words.
For Hrothgar soon a horse was saddled
1400
wave-maned steed. The sovran wise
stately rode on; his shield-armed men
followed in force. The footprints led
along the woodland, widely seen,
a path o'er the plain, where she passed, and trod
1405
the murky moor; of men-at-arms
she bore the bravest and best one, dead,
him who with Hrothgar the homestead ruled.
On then went the atheling-born
o'er stone-cliffs steep and strait defiles,
1410
narrow passes and unknown ways,
headlands sheer, and the haunts of the Nicors.
Foremost he {62} fared, a few at his side
of the wiser men, the ways to scan,
till he found in a flash the forested hill
1415
hanging over the hoary rock,

wynleasne wudu;   wæter under stod
dreorig ond gedrefed.   Denum eallum wæs,
winum Scyldinga,   weorce on mode
to geþolianne,   ðegne monegum,
1420
oncyð eorla gehwæm,   syðþan æscheres
on þam holmclife   hafelan metton.
Flod blode weol   (folc to sægon),
hatan heolfre.   Horn stundum song
fuslic fyrdleoð.   Feþa eal gesæt.
1425
Gesawon ða æfter wætere   wyrmcynnes fela,
sellice sædracan,   sund cunnian,
swylce on næshleoðum   nicras licgean,
ða on undernmæl   oft bewitigað
sorhfulne sið   on seglrade,
1430
wyrmas ond wildeor;   hie on weg hruron,
bitere ond gebolgne,   bearhtm ongeaton,
guðhorn galan.   Sumne Geata leod
of flanbogan   feores getwæfde,
yðgewinnes,   þæt him on aldre stod
1435
herestræl hearda;   he on holme wæs
sundes þe sænra,   ðe hyne swylt fornam.
Hræþe wearð on yðum   mid eoferspreotum
heorohocyhtum   hearde genearwod,
niða genæged,   ond on næs togen,
1440
wundorlic wægbora;   weras sceawedon
gryrelicne gist.   Gyrede hine Beowulf
eorlgewædum,   nalles for ealdre mearn.
Scolde herebyrne   hondum gebroden,
sid ond searofah,   sund cunnian,
1445
seo ðe bancofan   beorgan cuþe,
þæt him hildegrap   hreþre ne mihte,
eorres inwitfeng,   aldre gesceþðan;
ac se hwita helm   hafelan werede,
se þe meregrundas   mengan scolde,
1450
secan sundgebland   since geweorðad,
befongen freawrasnum,   swa hine fyrndagum

a woful wood: the waves below
were dyed in blood. The Danish men
had sorrow of soul, and for Scyldings all,
for many a hero, 'twas hard to bear,
1420
ill for earls, when Aeschere's head
they found by the flood on the foreland there.
Waves were welling, the warriors saw,
hot with blood; but the horn sang oft
battle-song bold. The band sat down,
1425
and watched on the water worm-like things,
sea-dragons strange that sounded the deep,
and nicors that lay on the ledge of the ness --
such as oft essay at hour of morn
on the road-of-sails their ruthless quest, --
1430
and sea-snakes and monsters. These started away,
swollen and savage that song to hear,
that war-horn's blast. The warden of Geats,
with bolt from bow, then balked of life,
of wave-work, one monster, amid its heart
1435
went the keen war-shaft; in water it seemed
less doughty in swimming whom death had seized.
Swift on the billows, with boar-spears well
hooked and barbed, it was hard beset,
done to death and dragged on the headland,
1440
wave-roamer wondrous. Warriors viewed
the grisly guest.
Then girt him Beowulf
in martial mail, nor mourned for his life.
His breastplate broad and bright of hues,
1445
woven by hand, should the waters try;
well could it ward the warrior's body
that battle should break on his breast in vain
nor harm his heart by the hand of a foe.
And the helmet white that his head protected
1450
was destined to dare the deeps of the flood,
through wave-whirl win: 'twas wound with chains,

worhte wæpna smið,   wundrum teode,
besette swinlicum,   þæt hine syðþan no
brond ne beadomecas   bitan ne meahton.
1455
Næs þæt þonne mætost   mægenfultuma
þæt him on ðearfe lah   ðyle Hroðgares;
wæs þæm hæftmece   Hrunting nama.
þæt wæs an foran   ealdgestreona;
ecg wæs iren,   atertanum fah,
1460
ahyrded heaþoswate;   næfre hit æt hilde ne swac
manna ængum   þara þe hit mid mundum bewand,
se ðe gryresiðas   gegan dorste,
folcstede fara;   næs þæt forma sið
þæt hit ellenweorc   æfnan scolde.
1465
Huru ne gemunde   mago Ecglafes,
eafoþes cræftig,   þæt he ær gespræc
wine druncen,   þa he þæs wæpnes onlah
selran sweordfrecan.   Selfa ne dorste
under yða gewin   aldre geneþan,
1470
drihtscype dreogan;   þær he dome forleas,
ellenmærðum.   Ne wæs þæm oðrum swa,
syðþan he hine to guðe   gegyred hæfde.

decked with gold, as in days of yore
the weapon-smith worked it wondrously,
with swine-forms set it, that swords nowise,
1455
brandished in battle, could bite that helm.
Nor was that the meanest of mighty helps
which Hrothgar's orator offered at need:
"Hrunting" they named the hilted sword,
of old-time heirlooms easily first;
1460
iron was its edge, all etched with poison,
with battle-blood hardened, nor blenched it at fight
in hero's hand who held it ever,
on paths of peril prepared to go
to folkstead {63} of foes. Not first time this
1465
it was destined to do a daring task.
For he bore not in mind, the bairn of Ecglaf
sturdy and strong, that speech he had made,
drunk with wine, now this weapon he lent
to a stouter swordsman. Himself, though, durst not
1470
under welter of waters wager his life
as loyal liegeman. So lost he his glory,
honor of earls. With the other not so,
who girded him now for the grim encounter.

Beowulf maðelode,   bearn Ecgþeowes:
"Geþenc nu, se mæra   maga Healfdenes,
1475
snottra fengel,   nu ic eom siðes fus,
goldwine gumena,   hwæt wit geo spræcon,
gif ic æt þearfe   þinre scolde
aldre linnan,   þæt ðu me a wære
forðgewitenum   on fæder stæle.
1480
Wes þu mundbora   minum magoþegnum,
hondgesellum,   gif mec hild nime;
swylce þu ða madmas   þe þu me sealdest,
Hroðgar leofa,   Higelace onsend.
Mæg þonne on þæm golde ongitan   Geata dryhten,
1485
geseon sunu Hrædles,   þonne he on þæt sinc
starað,
þæt ic gumcystum   godne funde
beaga bryttan,   breac þonne moste.
Ond þu Unferð læt   ealde lafe,
wrætlic wægsweord,   widcuðne man
1490
heardecg habban;   ic me mid Hruntinge
dom gewyrce,   oþðe mec deað nimeð."
æfter þæm wordum   Wedergeata leod
efste mid elne,   nalas ondsware
bidan wolde;   brimwylm onfeng
1495
hilderince.   ða wæs hwil dæges
ær he þone grundwong   ongytan mehte.
Sona þæt onfunde   se ðe floda begong
heorogifre beheold   hund missera,
grim ond grædig,   þæt þær gumena sum
1500
ælwihta eard   ufan cunnode.
Grap þa togeanes,   guðrinc gefeng
atolan clommum.   No þy ær in gescod
halan lice;   hring utan ymbbearh,
þæt heo þone fyrdhom   ðurhfon ne mihte,
1505
locene leoðosyrcan   laþan fingrum.

XXIII. THE BATTLE WITH THE WATER-DRAKE.

BEOWULF spake, bairn of Ecgtheow: --
"Have mind, thou honored offspring of Healfdene
1475
gold-friend of men, now I go on this quest,
sovran wise, what once was said:
if in thy cause it came that I
should lose my life, thou wouldst loyal bide
to me, though fallen, in father's place!
1480
Be guardian, thou, to this group of my thanes,
my warrior-friends, if War should seize me;
and the goodly gifts thou gavest me,
Hrothgar beloved, to Hygelac send!
Geatland's king may ken by the gold,
1485
Hrethel's son see, when he stares at the treasure,
that I got me a friend for goodness famed,
and joyed while I could in my jewel-bestower.
And let Unferth wield this wondrous sword,
earl far-honored, this heirloom precious,
1490
hard of edge: with Hrunting I
seek doom of glory, or Death shall take me."
After these words the Weder-Geat lord
boldly hastened, biding never
answer at all: the ocean floods
1495
closed o'er the hero. Long while of the day
fled ere he felt the floor of the sea.
Soon found the fiend who the flood-domain
sword-hungry held these hundred winters,
greedy and grim, that some guest from above,
1500
some man, was raiding her monster-realm.
She grasped out for him with grisly claws,
and the warrior seized; yet scathed she not
his body hale; the breastplate hindered,
as she strove to shatter the sark of war,
1505
the linked harness, with loathsome hand.

Bær þa seo brimwylf,   þa heo to botme com,
hringa þengel   to hofe sinum,
swa he ne mihte,   no he þæs modig wæs,
wæpna gewealdan,   ac hine wundra þæs fela
1510
swencte on sunde,   sædeor monig
hildetuxum   heresyrcan bræc,
ehton aglæcan.   ða se eorl ongeat
þæt he in niðsele   nathwylcum wæs,
þær him nænig wæter   wihte ne sceþede,
1515
ne him for hrofsele   hrinan ne mehte
færgripe flodes;   fyrleoht geseah,
blacne leoman,   beorhte scinan.
Ongeat þa se goda   grundwyrgenne,
merewif mihtig;   mægenræs forgeaf
1520
hildebille,   hond sweng ne ofteah,
þæt hire on hafelan   hringmæl agol
grædig guðleoð.   ða se gist onfand
þæt se beadoleoma   bitan nolde,
aldre sceþðan,   ac seo ecg geswac
1525
ðeodne æt þearfe;   ðolode ær fela
hondgemota,   helm oft gescær,
fæges fyrdhrægl;   ða wæs forma sið
deorum madme,   þæt his dom alæg.
Eft wæs anræd,   nalas elnes læt,
1530
mærða gemyndig   mæg Hylaces.
Wearp ða wundenmæl   wrættum gebunden
yrre oretta,   þæt hit on eorðan læg,
stið ond stylecg;   strenge getruwode,
mundgripe mægenes.   Swa sceal man don,
1535
þonne he æt guðe   gegan þenceð
longsumne lof,   na ymb his lif cearað.
Gefeng þa be eaxle   (nalas for fæhðe mearn)
Guðgeata leod   Grendles modor;
brægd þa beadwe heard,   þa he gebolgen wæs,
1540
feorhgeniðlan,   þæt heo on flet gebeah.
Heo him eft hraþe   andlean forgeald

Then bore this brine-wolf, when bottom she touched,
the lord of rings to the lair she haunted
whiles vainly he strove, though his valor held,
weapon to wield against wondrous monsters
1510
that sore beset him; sea-beasts many
tried with fierce tusks to tear his mail,
and swarmed on the stranger. But soon he marked
he was now in some hall, he knew not which,
where water never could work him harm,
1515
nor through the roof could reach him ever
fangs of the flood. Firelight he saw,
beams of a blaze that brightly shone.
Then the warrior was ware of that wolf-of-the-deep,
mere-wife monstrous. For mighty stroke
1520
he swung his blade, and the blow withheld not.
Then sang on her head that seemly blade
its war-song wild. But the warrior found
the light-of-battle {64} was loath to bite,
to harm the heart: its hard edge failed
1525
the noble at need, yet had known of old
strife hand to hand, and had helmets cloven,
doomed men's fighting-gear. First time, this,
for the gleaming blade that its glory fell.
Firm still stood, nor failed in valor,
1530
heedful of high deeds, Hygelac's kinsman;
flung away fretted sword, featly jewelled,
the angry earl; on earth it lay
steel-edged and stiff. His strength he trusted,
hand-gripe of might. So man shall do
1535
whenever in war he weens to earn him
lasting fame, nor fears for his life!
Seized then by shoulder, shrank not from combat,
the Geatish war-prince Grendel's mother.
Flung then the fierce one, filled with wrath,
1540
his deadly foe, that she fell to ground.
Swift on her part she paid him back

grimman grapum   ond him togeanes feng;
oferwearp þa werigmod   wigena strengest,
feþecempa,   þæt he on fylle wearð.
1545
Ofsæt þa þone selegyst   ond hyre seax geteah,
brad ond brunecg,   wolde hire bearn wrecan,
angan eaferan.   Him on eaxle læg
breostnet broden;   þæt gebearh feore,
wið ord ond wið ecge   ingang forstod.
1550
Hæfde ða forsiðod   sunu Ecgþeowes
under gynne grund,   Geata cempa,
nemne him heaðobyrne   helpe gefremede,
herenet hearde,   ond halig god
geweold wigsigor;   witig drihten,
1555
rodera rædend,   hit on ryht gesced
yðelice,   syþðan he eft astod.

with grisly grasp, and grappled with him.
Spent with struggle, stumbled the warrior,
fiercest of fighting-men, fell adown.
1545
On the hall-guest she hurled herself, hent her short
sword,
broad and brown-edged, {65} the bairn to avenge,
the sole-born son. -- On his shoulder lay
braided breast-mail, barring death,
withstanding entrance of edge or blade.
1550
Life would have ended for Ecgtheow's son,
under wide earth for that earl of Geats,
had his armor of war not aided him,
battle-net hard, and holy God
wielded the victory, wisest Maker.
1555
The Lord of Heaven allowed his cause;
and easily rose the earl erect.

Geseah ða on searwum   sigeeadig bil,
eald sweord eotenisc,   ecgum þyhtig,
wigena weorðmynd;   þæt wæs wæpna cyst,
1560
buton hit wæs mare   ðonne ænig mon oðer
to beadulace   ætberan meahte,
god ond geatolic,   giganta geweorc.
He gefeng þa fetelhilt,   freca Scyldinga
hreoh ond heorogrim   hringmæl gebrægd,
1565
aldres orwena,   yrringa sloh,
þæt hire wið halse   heard grapode,
banhringas bræc.   Bil eal ðurhwod
fægne flæschoman;   heo on flet gecrong.
Sweord wæs swatig,   secg weorce gefeh.
1570
Lixte se leoma,   leoht inne stod,
efne swa of hefene   hadre scineð
rodores candel.   He æfter recede wlat;
hwearf þa be wealle,   wæpen hafenade
heard be hiltum   Higelaces ðegn,
1575
yrre ond anræd.   Næs seo ecg fracod
hilderince,   ac he hraþe wolde
Grendle forgyldan   guðræsa fela
ðara þe he geworhte   to Westdenum
oftor micle   ðonne on ænne sið,
1580
þonne he Hroðgares   heorðgeneatas
sloh on sweofote,   slæpende fræt
folces Denigea   fyftyne men
ond oðer swylc   ut offerede,
laðlicu lac.   He him þæs lean forgeald,
1585
reþe cempa,   to ðæs þe he on ræste geseah
guðwerigne   Grendel licgan
aldorleasne,   swa him ær gescod
hild æt Heorote.   Hra wide sprong,
syþðan he æfter deaðe   drepe þrowade,
1590
heorosweng heardne,   ond hine þa heafde becearf.

XXIV. BEOWULF SLAYS THE SPRITE.

'MID the battle-gear saw he a blade triumphant,
old-sword of Eotens, with edge of proof,
warriors' heirloom, weapon unmatched,
1560
-- save only 'twas more than other men
to bandy-of-battle could bear at all --
as the giants had wrought it, ready and keen.
Seized then its chain-hilt the Scyldings' chieftain,
bold and battle-grim, brandished the sword,
1565
reckless of life, and so wrathfully smote
that it gripped her neck and grasped her hard,
her bone-rings breaking: the blade pierced through
that fated-one's flesh: to floor she sank.
Bloody the blade: he was blithe of his deed.
1570
Then blazed forth light. 'Twas bright within
as when from the sky there shines unclouded
heaven's candle. The hall he scanned.
By the wall then went he; his weapon raised
high by its hilts the Hygelac-thane,
1575
angry and eager. That edge was not useless
to the warrior now. He wished with speed
Grendel to guerdon for grim raids many,
for the war he waged on Western-Danes
oftener far than an only time,
1580
when of Hrothgar's hearth-companions
he slew in slumber, in sleep devoured,
fifteen men of the folk of Danes,
and as many others outward bore,
his horrible prey. Well paid for that
1585
the wrathful prince! For now prone he saw
Grendel stretched there, spent with war,
spoiled of life, so scathed had left him
Heorot's battle. The body sprang far
when after death it endured the blow,
1590
sword-stroke savage, that severed its head.

Sona þæt gesawon   snottre ceorlas,
þa ðe mid Hroðgare   on holm wliton,
þæt wæs yðgeblond   eal gemenged,
brim blode fah.   Blondenfeaxe,
1595
gomele ymb godne,   ongeador spræcon
þæt hig þæs æðelinges   eft ne wendon
þæt he sigehreðig   secean come
mærne þeoden;   þa ðæs monige gewearð
þæt hine seo brimwylf   abroten hæfde.
1600
ða com non dæges.   Næs ofgeafon
hwate Scyldingas;   gewat him ham þonon
goldwine gumena.   Gistas setan
modes seoce   ond on mere staredon,
wiston ond ne wendon   þæt hie heora winedrihten
1605
selfne gesawon.   þa þæt sweord ongan
æfter heaþoswate   hildegicelum,
wigbil wanian.   þæt wæs wundra sum,
þæt hit eal gemealt   ise gelicost,
ðonne forstes bend   fæder onlæteð,
1610
onwindeð wælrapas,   se geweald hafað
sæla ond mæla;   þæt is soð metod.
Ne nom he in þæm wicum,   Wedergeata leod,
maðmæhta ma,   þeh he þær monige geseah,
buton þone hafelan   ond þa hilt somod
1615
since fage.   Sweord ær gemealt,
forbarn brodenmæl;   wæs þæt blod to þæs hat,
ættren ellorgæst   se þær inne swealt.
Sona wæs on sunde   se þe ær æt sæcce gebad
wighryre wraðra,   wæter up þurhdeaf.
1620
Wæron yðgebland   eal gefælsod,
eacne eardas,   þa se ellorgast
oflet lifdagas   ond þas lænan gesceaft.
Com þa to lande   lidmanna helm
swiðmod swymman;   sælace gefeah,
1625
mægenbyrþenne   þara þe he him mid hæfde.
Eodon him þa togeanes,   gode þancodon,

Soon, {66} then, saw the sage companions
who waited with Hrothgar, watching the flood,
that the tossing waters turbid grew,
blood-stained the mere. Old men together,
1595
hoary-haired, of the hero spake;
the warrior would not, they weened, again,
proud of conquest, come to seek
their mighty master. To many it seemed
the wolf-of-the-waves had won his life.
1600
The ninth hour came. The noble Scyldings
left the headland; homeward went
the gold-friend of men. {67} But the guests sat on,
stared at the surges, sick in heart,
and wished, yet weened not, their winsome lord
1605
again to see. Now that sword began,
from blood of the fight, in battle-droppings, {68}
war-blade, to wane: 'twas a wondrous thing
that all of it melted as ice is wont
when frosty fetters the Father loosens,
1610
unwinds the wave-bonds, wielding all
seasons and times: the true God he!
Nor took from that dwelling the duke of the Geats
precious things, though a plenty he saw,
save only the head and that hilt withal
1615
blazoned with jewels: the blade had melted,
burned was the bright sword, her blood was so hot,
so poisoned the hell-sprite who perished within there.
Soon he was swimming who safe saw in combat
downfall of demons; up-dove through the flood.
1620
The clashing waters were cleansed now,
waste of waves, where the wandering fiend
her life-days left and this lapsing world.
Swam then to strand the sailors'-refuge,
sturdy-in-spirit, of sea-booty glad,
1625
of burden brave he bore with him.
Went then to greet him, and God they thanked,

ðryðlic þegna heap,   þeodnes gefegon,
þæs þe hi hyne gesundne   geseon moston.
ða wæs of þæm hroran   helm ond byrne
1630
lungre alysed.   Lagu drusade,
wæter under wolcnum,   wældreore fag.
Ferdon forð þonon   feþelastum
ferhþum fægne,   foldweg mæton,
cuþe stræte.   Cyningbalde men
1635
from þæm holmclife   hafelan bæron
earfoðlice   heora æghwæþrum,
felamodigra;   feower scoldon
on þæm wælstenge   weorcum geferian
to þæm goldsele   Grendles heafod,
1640
oþðæt semninga   to sele comon
frome fyrdhwate   feowertyne
Geata gongan;   gumdryhten mid
modig on gemonge   meodowongas træd.
ða com in gan   ealdor ðegna,
1645
dædcene mon   dome gewurþad,
hæle hildedeor,   Hroðgar gretan.
þa wæs be feaxe   on flet boren
Grendles heafod,   þær guman druncon,
egeslic for eorlum   ond þære idese mid,
1650
wliteseon wrætlic;   weras on sawon.

the thane-band choice of their chieftain blithe,
that safe and sound they could see him again.
Soon from the hardy one helmet and armor
1630
deftly they doffed: now drowsed the mere,
water 'neath welkin, with war-blood stained.
Forth they fared by the footpaths thence,
merry at heart the highways measured,
well-known roads. Courageous men
1635
carried the head from the cliff by the sea,
an arduous task for all the band,
the firm in fight, since four were needed
on the shaft-of-slaughter {69} strenuously
to bear to the gold-hall Grendel's head.
1640
So presently to the palace there
foemen fearless, fourteen Geats,
marching came. Their master-of-clan
mighty amid them the meadow-ways trod.
Strode then within the sovran thane
1645
fearless in fight, of fame renowned,
hardy hero, Hrothgar to greet.
And next by the hair into hall was borne
Grendel's head, where the henchmen were drinking,
an awe to clan and queen alike,
1650
a monster of marvel: the men looked on.

Beowulf maþelode,   bearn Ecgþeowes:
"Hwæt! we þe þas sælac,   sunu Healfdenes,
leod Scyldinga,   lustum brohton
tires to tacne,   þe þu her to locast.
1655
Ic þæt unsofte   ealdre gedigde
wigge under wætere,   weorc geneþde
earfoðlice;   ætrihte wæs
guð getwæfed,   nymðe mec god scylde.
Ne meahte ic æt hilde   mid Hruntinge
1660
wiht gewyrcan,   þeah þæt wæpen duge;
ac me geuðe   ylda waldend
þæt ic on wage geseah   wlitig hangian
eald sweord eacen   (oftost wisode
winigea leasum),   þæt ic ðy wæpne gebræd.
1665
Ofsloh ða æt þære sæcce,   þa me sæl ageald,
huses hyrdas.   þa þæt hildebil
forbarn brogdenmæl,   swa þæt blod gesprang,
hatost heaþoswata.   Ic þæt hilt þanan
feondum ætferede,   fyrendæda wræc,
1670
deaðcwealm Denigea,   swa hit gedefe wæs.
Ic hit þe þonne gehate,   þæt þu on Heorote most
sorhleas swefan   mid þinra secga gedryht
ond þegna gehwylc   þinra leoda,
duguðe ond iogoþe,   þæt þu him ondrædan ne
þearft,
1675
þeoden Scyldinga,   on þa healfe,
aldorbealu eorlum,   swa þu ær dydest."
ða wæs gylden hilt   gamelum rince,
harum hildfruman,   on hand gyfen,
enta ærgeweorc;   hit on æht gehwearf
1680
æfter deofla hryre   Denigea frean,
wundorsmiþa geweorc,   ond þa þas worold ofgeaf
gromheort guma,   godes ondsaca,
morðres scyldig,   ond his modor eac,
on geweald gehwearf   woroldcyninga

XXV. HROTHGAR'S GRATITUDE: HE DISCOURSES.

BEOWULF spake, bairn of Ecgtheow: --
"Lo, now, this sea-booty, son of Healfdene,
Lord of Scyldings, we've lustily brought thee,
sign of glory; thou seest it here.
1655
Not lightly did I with my life escape!
In war under water this work I essayed
with endless effort; and even so
my strength had been lost had the Lord not shielded me.
Not a whit could I with Hrunting do
1660
in work of war, though the weapon is good;
yet a sword the Sovran of Men vouchsafed me
to spy on the wall there, in splendor hanging,
old, gigantic, -- how oft He guides
the friendless wight! -- and I fought with that brand,
1665
felling in fight, since fate was with me,
the house's wardens. That war-sword then
all burned, bright blade, when the blood gushed o'er it,
battle-sweat hot; but the hilt I brought back
from my foes. So avenged I their fiendish deeds
1670
death-fall of Danes, as was due and right.
And this is my hest, that in Heorot now
safe thou canst sleep with thy soldier band,
and every thane of all thy folk
both old and young; no evil fear,
1675
Scyldings' lord, from that side again,
aught ill for thy earls, as erst thou must!"
Then the golden hilt, for that gray-haired leader,
hoary hero, in hand was laid,
giant-wrought, old. So owned and enjoyed it
1680
after downfall of devils, the Danish lord,
wonder-smiths' work, since the world was rid
of that grim-souled fiend, the foe of God,
murder-marked, and his mother as well.
Now it passed into power of the people's king,

1685
ðæm selestan   be sæm tweonum
ðara þe on Scedenigge   sceattas dælde.
Hroðgar maðelode,   hylt sceawode,
ealde lafe,   on ðæm wæs or writen
fyrngewinnes,   syðþan flod ofsloh,
1690
gifen geotende,   giganta cyn
(frecne geferdon);   þæt wæs fremde þeod
ecean dryhtne;   him þæs endelean
þurh wæteres wylm   waldend sealde.
Swa wæs on ðæm scennum   sciran goldes
1695
þurh runstafas   rihte gemearcod,
geseted ond gesæd   hwam þæt sweord geworht,
irena cyst,   ærest wære,
wreoþenhilt ond wyrmfah.   ða se wisa spræc
sunu Healfdenes   (swigedon ealle):
1700
"þæt, la, mæg secgan   se þe soð ond riht
fremeð on folce,   feor eal gemon,
eald weard,   þæt ðes eorl wære
geboren betera!   Blæd is aræred
geond widwegas,   wine min Beowulf,
1705
ðin ofer þeoda gehwylce.   Eal þu hit geþyldum
healdest,
mægen mid modes snyttrum.   Ic þe sceal mine
gelæstan
freode, swa wit furðum spræcon.   ðu scealt to frofre
weorþan
eal langtwidig   leodum þinum,
hæleðum to helpe.   Ne wearð Heremod swa
1710
eaforum Ecgwelan,   Arscyldingum;
ne geweox he him to willan,   ac to wælfealle
ond to deaðcwalum   Deniga leodum;
breat bolgenmod   beodgeneatas,
eaxlgesteallan,   oþþæt he ana hwearf,
1715
mære þeoden,   mondreamum from.
ðeah þe hine mihtig god   mægenes wynnum,
eafeþum stepte,   ofer ealle men

1685
best of all that the oceans bound
who have scattered their gold o'er Scandia's isle.
Hrothgar spake -- the hilt he viewed,
heirloom old, where was etched the rise
of that far-off fight when the floods o'erwhelmed,
1690
raging waves, the race of giants
(fearful their fate!), a folk estranged
from God Eternal: whence guerdon due
in that waste of waters the Wielder paid them.
So on the guard of shining gold
1695
in runic staves it was rightly said
for whom the serpent-traced sword was wrought,
best of blades, in bygone days,
and the hilt well wound. -- The wise-one spake,
son of Healfdene; silent were all: --
1700
"Lo, so may he say who sooth and right
follows 'mid folk, of far times mindful,
a land-warden old, {70} that this earl belongs
to the better breed! So, borne aloft,
thy fame must fly, O friend my Beowulf,
1705
far and wide o'er folksteads many. Firmly thou
shalt all maintain,
mighty strength with mood of wisdom. Love of
mine will I assure thee,
as, awhile ago, I promised; thou shalt prove a stay
in future,
in far-off years, to folk of thine,
to the heroes a help. Was not Heremod thus
1710
to offspring of Ecgwela, Honor-Scyldings,
nor grew for their grace, but for grisly slaughter,
for doom of death to the Danishmen.
He slew, wrath-swollen, his shoulder-comrades,
companions at board! So he passed alone,
1715
chieftain haughty, from human cheer.
Though him the Maker with might endowed,
delights of power, and uplifted high

forð gefremede,   hwæþere him on ferhþe greow
breosthord blodreow.   Nallas beagas geaf
1720
Denum æfter dome;   dreamleas gebad
þæt he þæs gewinnes   weorc þrowade,
leodbealo longsum.   ðu þe lær be þon,
gumcyste ongit;   ic þis gid be þe
awræc wintrum frod.   Wundor is to secganne
1725
hu mihtig god   manna cynne
þurh sidne sefan   snyttru bryttað,
eard ond eorlscipe;   he ah ealra geweald.
Hwilum he on lufan   læteð hworfan
monnes modgeþonc   mæran cynnes,
1730
seleð him on eþle   eorþan wynne
to healdanne,   hleoburh wera,
gedeð him swa gewealdene   worolde dælas,
side rice,   þæt he his selfa ne mæg
for his unsnyttrum   ende geþencean.
1735
Wunað he on wiste;   no hine wiht dweleð
adl ne yldo,   ne him inwitsorh
on sefan sweorceð,   ne gesacu ohwær
ecghete eoweð,   ac him eal worold
wendeð on willan   (he þæt wyrse ne con),
1740
oðþæt him on innan   oferhygda dæl
weaxeð ond wridað.   þonne se weard swefeð,
sawele hyrde;   bið se slæp to fæst,
bisgum gebunden,   bona swiðe neah,
se þe of flanbogan   fyrenum sceoteð.

above all men, yet blood-fierce his mind,
his breast-hoard, grew, no bracelets gave he
1720
to Danes as was due; he endured all joyless
strain of struggle and stress of woe,
long feud with his folk. Here find thy lesson!
Of virtue advise thee! This verse I have said for thee,
wise from lapsed winters. Wondrous seems
1725
how to sons of men Almighty God
in the strength of His spirit sendeth wisdom,
estate, high station: He swayeth all things.
Whiles He letteth right lustily fare
the heart of the hero of high-born race, --
1730
in seat ancestral assigns him bliss,
his folk's sure fortress in fee to hold,
puts in his power great parts of the earth,
empire so ample, that end of it
this wanter-of-wisdom weeneth none.
1735
So he waxes in wealth, nowise can harm him
illness or age; no evil cares
shadow his spirit; no sword-hate threatens
from ever an enemy: all the world
wends at his will, no worse he knoweth,
1740
till all within him obstinate pride
waxes and wakes while the warden slumbers,
the spirit's sentry; sleep is too fast
which masters his might, and the murderer nears,
stealthily shooting the shafts from his bow!

1745
þonne bið on hreþre   under helm drepen
biteran stræle   (him bebeorgan ne con),
wom wundorbebodum   wergan gastes;
þinceð him to lytel   þæt he lange heold,
gytsað gromhydig,   nallas on gylp seleð
1750
fædde beagas,   ond he þa forðgesceaft
forgyteð ond forgymeð,   þæs þe him ær god sealde,
wuldres waldend,   weorðmynda dæl.
Hit on endestæf   eft gelimpeð
þæt se lichoma   læne gedreoseð,
1755
fæge gefealleð;   fehð oþer to,
se þe unmurnlice   madmas dæleþ,
eorles ærgestreon,   egesan ne gymeð.
Bebeorh þe ðone bealonið,   Beowulf leofa,
secg betsta,   ond þe þæt selre geceos,
1760
ece rædas;   oferhyda ne gym,
mære cempa.   Nu is þines mægnes blæd
ane hwile.   Eft sona bið
þæt þec adl oððe ecg   eafoþes getwæfeð,
oððe fyres feng,   oððe flodes wylm,
1765
oððe gripe meces,   oððe gares fliht,
oððe atol yldo;   oððe eagena bearhtm
forsiteð ond forsworceð;   semninga bið
þæt ðec, dryhtguma,   dead oferswyðeð.
Swa ic Hringdena   hund missera
1770
weold under wolcnum   ond hig wigge beleac
manigum mægþa   geond þysne middangeard,
æscum ond ecgum,   þæt ic me ænigne
under swegles begong   gesacan ne tealde.
Hwæt, me þæs on eþle   edwenden cwom,
1775
gyrn æfter gomene,   seoþðan Grendel wearð,
ealdgewinna,   ingenga min;
ic þære socne   singales wæg

XXVI. THE DISCOURSE IS ENDED.
-BEOWULF PREPARES TO LEAVE.

1745
"UNDER harness his heart then is hit indeed
by sharpest shafts; and no shelter avails
from foul behest of the hellish fiend. {71}
Him seems too little what long he possessed.
Greedy and grim, no golden rings
1750
he gives for his pride; the promised future
forgets he and spurns, with all God has sent him,
Wonder-Wielder, of wealth and fame.
Yet in the end it ever comes
that the frame of the body fragile yields,
1755
fated falls; and there follows another
who joyously the jewels divides,
the royal riches, nor recks of his forebear.
Ban, then, such baleful thoughts, Beowulf dearest,
best of men, and the better part choose,
1760
profit eternal; and temper thy pride,
warrior famous! The flower of thy might
lasts now a while: but erelong it shall be
that sickness or sword thy strength shall minish,
or fang of fire, or flooding billow,
1765
or bite of blade, or brandished spear,
or odious age; or the eyes' clear beam
wax dull and darken: Death even thee
in haste shall o'erwhelm, thou hero of war!
So the Ring-Danes these half-years a hundred I ruled,
1770
wielded 'neath welkin, and warded them bravely
from mighty-ones many o'er middle-earth,
from spear and sword, till it seemed for me
no foe could be found under fold of the sky.
Lo, sudden the shift! To me seated secure
1775
came grief for joy when Grendel began
to harry my home, the hellish foe;
for those ruthless raids, unresting I suffered

modceare micle.   þæs sig metode þanc,
ecean dryhtne,   þæs ðe ic on aldre gebad
1780
þæt ic on þone hafelan   heorodreorigne
ofer ealdgewin   eagum starige!
Ga nu to setle,   symbelwynne dreoh
wigge weorþad;   unc sceal worn fela
maþma gemænra,   siþðan morgen bið."
1785
Geat wæs glædmod,   geong sona to
setles neosan,   swa se snottra heht.
þa wæs eft swa ær   ellenrofum
fletsittendum   fægere gereorded
niowan stefne.   Nihthelm geswearc
1790
deorc ofer dryhtgumum.   Duguð eal aras.
Wolde blondenfeax   beddes neosan,
gamela Scylding.   Geat unigmetes wel,
rofne randwigan,   restan lyste;
sona him seleþegn   siðes wergum,
1795
feorrancundum,   forð wisade,
se for andrysnum   ealle beweotede
þegnes þearfe,   swylce þy dogore
heaþoliðende   habban scoldon.
Reste hine þa rumheort;   reced hliuade
1800
geap ond goldfah;   gæst inne swæf
oþþæt hrefn blaca   heofones wynne
bliðheort bodode.   ða com beorht scacan
    scaþan onetton,
wæron æþelingas   eft to leodum
1805
fuse to farenne;   wolde feor þanon
cuma collenferhð   ceoles neosan.
Heht þa se hearda   Hrunting beran
sunu Ecglafes,   heht his sweord niman,
leoflic iren;   sægde him þæs leanes þanc,
1810
cwæð, he þone guðwine   godne tealde,
wigcræftigne,   nales wordum log
meces ecge;   þæt wæs modig secg.
Ond þa siðfrome,   searwum gearwe

heart-sorrow heavy. Heaven be thanked,
Lord Eternal, for life extended
1780
that I on this head all hewn and bloody,
after long evil, with eyes may gaze!
-- Go to the bench now! Be glad at banquet,
warrior worthy! A wealth of treasure
at dawn of day, be dealt between us!"
1785
Glad was the Geats' lord, going betimes
to seek his seat, as the Sage commanded.
Afresh, as before, for the famed-in-battle,
for the band of the hall, was a banquet dight
nobly anew. The Night-Helm darkened
1790
dusk o'er the drinkers. The doughty ones rose:
for the hoary-headed would hasten to rest,
aged Scylding; and eager the Geat,
shield-fighter sturdy, for sleeping yearned.
Him wander-weary, warrior-guest
1795
from far, a hall-thane heralded forth,
who by custom courtly cared for all
needs of a thane as in those old days
warrior-wanderers wont to have.
So slumbered the stout-heart. Stately the hall
1800
rose gabled and gilt where the guest slept on
till a raven black the rapture-of-heaven {72}
blithe-heart boded. Bright came flying
shine after shadow. The swordsmen hastened,
athelings all were eager homeward
1805
forth to fare; and far from thence
the great-hearted guest would guide his keel.
Bade then the hardy-one Hrunting be brought
to the son of Ecglaf, the sword bade him take,
excellent iron, and uttered his thanks for it,
1810
quoth that he counted it keen in battle,
"war-friend" winsome: with words he slandered not
edge of the blade: 'twas a big-hearted man!
Now eager for parting and armed at point

wigend wæron;   eode weorð Denum
1815
æþeling to yppan,   þær se oþer wæs,
hæle hildedeor   Hroðgar grette.

warriors waited, while went to his host
1815
that Darling of Danes. The doughty atheling
to high-seat hastened and Hrothgar greeted.

Beowulf maþelode,   bearn Ecgþeowes:
"Nu we sæliðend   secgan wyllað,
feorran cumene,   þæt we fundiaþ
1820
Higelac secan.   Wæron her tela
willum bewenede;   þu us wel dohtest.
Gif ic þonne on eorþan   owihte mæg
þinre modlufan   maran tilian,
gumena dryhten,   ðonne ic gyt dyde,
1825
guðgeweorca,   ic beo gearo sona.
Gif ic þæt gefricge   ofer floda begang,
þæt þec ymbsittend   egesan þywað,
swa þec hetende   hwilum dydon,
ic ðe þusenda   þegna bringe,
1830
hæleþa to helpe.   Ic on Higelac wat,
Geata dryhten,   þeah ðe he geong sy,
folces hyrde,   þæt he mec fremman wile
wordum ond worcum,   þæt ic þe wel herige
ond þe to geoce   garholt bere,
1835
mægenes fultum,   þær ðe bið manna þearf.
Gif him þonne Hreþric   to hofum Geata
geþingeð, þeodnes bearn,   he mæg þær fela
freonda findan;   feorcyþðe beoð
selran gesohte   þæm þe him selfa deah."

1840
Hroðgar maþelode   him on ondsware:
"þe þa wordcwydas   wigtig drihten
on sefan sende;   ne hyrde ic snotorlicor
on swa geongum feore   guman þingian.
þu eart mægenes strang   ond on mode frod,
1845
wis wordcwida.   Wen ic talige,
gif þæt gegangeð,   þæt ðe gar nymeð,
hild heorugrimme,   Hreþles eaferan,
adl oþðe iren   ealdor ðinne,
folces hyrde,   ond þu þin feorh hafast,

XXVII. THE PARTING WORDS.

BEOWULF spake, bairn of Ecgtheow: --
"Lo, we seafarers say our will,
far-come men, that we fain would seek
1820
Hygelac now. We here have found
hosts to our heart: thou hast harbored us well.
If ever on earth I am able to win me
more of thy love, O lord of men,
aught anew, than I now have done,
1825
for work of war I am willing still!
If it come to me ever across the seas
that neighbor foemen annoy and fright thee, --
as they that hate thee erewhile have used, --
thousands then of thanes I shall bring,
1830
heroes to help thee. Of Hygelac I know,
ward of his folk, that, though few his years,
the lord of the Geats will give me aid
by word and by work, that well I may serve thee,
wielding the war-wood to win thy triumph
1835
and lending thee might when thou lackest men.
If thy Hrethric should come to court of Geats,
a sovran's son, he will surely there
find his friends. A far-off land
each man should visit who vaunts him brave."

1840
Him then answering, Hrothgar spake: --
"These words of thine the wisest God
sent to thy soul! No sager counsel
from so young in years e'er yet have I heard.
Thou art strong of main and in mind art wary,
1845
art wise in words! I ween indeed
if ever it hap that Hrethel's heir
by spear be seized, by sword-grim battle,
by illness or iron, thine elder and lord,
people's leader, -- and life be thine, --

Beowulf

```
1850
þæt þe Sægeatas          selran næbben
to geceosenne      cyning ænigne,
hordweard hæleþa,        gyf þu healdan wylt
maga rice.     Me þin modsefa
licað leng swa wel,      leofa Beowulf.
1855
Hafast þu gefered        þæt þam folcum sceal,
Geata leodum       ond Gardenum,
sib gemæne,        ond sacu restan,
inwitniþas,        þe hie ær drugon,
wesan, þenden ic wealde        widan rices,
1860
maþmas gemæne,           manig oþerne
godum gegretan     ofer ganotes bæð;
sceal hringnaca    ofer heafu bringan
lac ond luftacen.      Ic þa leode wat
ge wið feond ge wið freond        fæste geworhte,
1865
æghwæs untæle      ealde wisan."
ða git him eorla hleo        inne gesealde,
mago Healfdenes,         maþmas XII;
het hine mid þæm lacum       leode swæse
secean on gesyntum,      snude eft cuman.
1870
Gecyste þa      cyning æþelum god,
þeoden Scyldinga,        ðegn betstan
ond be healse genam;     hruron him tearas,
blondenfeaxum.     Him wæs bega wen,
ealdum infrodum,         oþres swiðor,
1875
þæt hie seoððan no       geseon moston,
modige on meþle.       Wæs him se man to þon leof
þæt he þone breostwylm       forberan ne mehte,
ac him on hreþre        hygebendum fæst
æfter deorum men     dyrne langað
1880
beorn wið blode.       Him Beowulf þanan,
guðrinc goldwlanc,       græsmoldan træd
since hremig;      sægenga bad
agendfrean,      se þe on ancre rad.
þa wæs on gange       gifu Hroðgares
```

1850
no seemlier man will the Sea-Geats find
at all to choose for their chief and king,
for hoard-guard of heroes, if hold thou wilt
thy kinsman's kingdom! Thy keen mind pleases me
the longer the better, Beowulf loved!
1855
Thou hast brought it about that both our peoples,
sons of the Geat and Spear-Dane folk,
shall have mutual peace, and from murderous strife,
such as once they waged, from war refrain.
Long as I rule this realm so wide,
1860
let our hoards be common, let heroes with gold
each other greet o'er the gannet's-bath,
and the ringed-prow bear o'er rolling waves
tokens of love. I trow my landfolk
towards friend and foe are firmly joined,
1865
and honor they keep in the olden way."
To him in the hall, then, Healfdene's son
gave treasures twelve, and the trust-of-earls
bade him fare with the gifts to his folk beloved,
hale to his home, and in haste return.
1870
Then kissed the king of kin renowned,
Scyldings' chieftain, that choicest thane,
and fell on his neck. Fast flowed the tears
of the hoary-headed. Heavy with winters,
he had chances twain, but he clung to this, {73} --
1875
that each should look on the other again,
and hear him in hall. Was this hero so dear to him.
his breast's wild billows he banned in vain;
safe in his soul a secret longing,
locked in his mind, for that loved man
1880
burned in his blood. Then Beowulf strode,
glad of his gold-gifts, the grass-plot o'er,
warrior blithe. The wave-roamer bode
riding at anchor, its owner awaiting.
As they hastened onward, Hrothgar's gift

1885
oft geæhted;   þæt wæs an cyning,
æghwæs orleahtre,   oþþæt hine yldo benam
mægenes wynnum,   se þe oft manegum scod.

1885
they lauded at length. -- 'Twas a lord unpeered,
every way blameless, till age had broken
-- it spareth no mortal -- his splendid might.

Cwom þa to flode   felamodigra,
hægstealdra heap,   hringnet bæron,
1890
locene leoðosyrcan.   Landweard onfand
eftsið eorla,   swa he ær dyde;
no he mid hearme   of hliðes nosan
gæstas grette,   ac him togeanes rad,
cwæð þæt wilcuman   Wedera leodum
1895
scaþan scirhame   to scipe foron.
þa wæs on sande   sægeap naca
hladen herewædum,   hringedstefna,
mearum ond maðmum;   mæst hlifade
ofer Hroðgares   hordgestreonum.
1900
He þæm batwearde   bunden golde
swurd gesealde,   þæt he syðþan wæs
on meodubence   maþme þy weorþra,
yrfelafe.   Gewat him on naca
drefan deop wæter,   Dena land ofgeaf.
1905
þa wæs be mæste   merehrægla sum,
segl sale fæst;   sundwudu þunede.
No þær wegflotan   wind ofer yðum
siðes getwæfde;   sægenga for,
fleat famigheals   forð ofer yðe,
1910
bundenstefna   ofer brimstreamas,
þæt hie Geata clifu   ongitan meahton,
cuþe næssas.   Ceol up geþrang
lyftgeswenced,   on lande stod.
Hraþe wæs æt holme   hyðweard geara,
1915
se þe ær lange tid   leofra manna
fus æt faroðe   feor wlatode;
sælde to sande   sidfæþme scip,
oncerbendum fæst,   þy læs hym yþa ðrym
wudu wynsuman   forwrecan meahte.
1920
Het þa up beran   æþelinga gestreon,

142

XXVIII. BEOWULF RETURNS TO GEATLAND.
-THE QUEENS HYGD AND THRYTHO.

CAME now to ocean the ever-courageous
hardy henchmen, their harness bearing,
1890
woven war-sarks. The warden marked,
trusty as ever, the earl's return.
From the height of the hill no hostile words
reached the guests as he rode to greet them;
but "Welcome!" he called to that Weder clan
1895
as the sheen-mailed spoilers to ship marched on.
Then on the strand, with steeds and treasure
and armor their roomy and ring-dight ship
was heavily laden: high its mast
rose over Hrothgar's hoarded gems.
1900
A sword to the boat-guard Beowulf gave,
mounted with gold; on the mead-bench since
he was better esteemed, that blade possessing,
heirloom old. -- Their ocean-keel boarding,
they drove through the deep, and Daneland left.
1905
A sea-cloth was set, a sail with ropes,
firm to the mast; the flood-timbers moaned; {74}
nor did wind over billows that wave-swimmer blow
across from her course. The craft sped on,
foam-necked it floated forth o'er the waves,
1910
keel firm-bound over briny currents,
till they got them sight of the Geatish cliffs,
home-known headlands. High the boat,
stirred by winds, on the strand updrove.
Helpful at haven the harbor-guard stood,
1915
who long already for loved companions
by the water had waited and watched afar.
He bound to the beach the broad-bosomed ship
with anchor-bands, lest ocean-billows
that trusty timber should tear away.
1920
Then Beowulf bade them bear the treasure,

frætwe ond fætgold;   næs him feor þanon
to gesecanne   sinces bryttan,
Higelac Hreþling,   þær æt ham wunað
selfa mid gesiðum   sæwealle neah.
1925
Bold wæs betlic,   bregorof cyning,
heah in healle,   Hygd swiðe geong,
wis, welþungen,   þeah ðe wintra lyt
under burhlocan   gebiden hæbbe,
Hæreþes dohtor;   næs hio hnah swa þeah,
1930
ne to gneað gifa   Geata leodum,
maþmgestreona.   Mod þryðo wæg,
fremu folces cwen,   firen ondrysne.
Nænig þæt dorste   deor geneþan
swæsra gesiða,   nefne sinfrea,
1935
þæt hire an dæges   eagum starede,
ac him wælbende   weotode tealde
handgewriþene;   hraþe seoþðan wæs
æfter mundgripe   mece geþinged,
þæt hit sceadenmæl   scyran moste,
1940
cwealmbealu cyðan.   Ne bið swylc cwenlic þeaw
idese to efnanne,   þeah ðe hio ænlicu sy,
þætte freoðuwebbe   feores onsæce
æfter ligetorne   leofne mannan.
Huru þæt onhohsnode   Hemminges mæg;
1945
ealodrincende   oðer sædan,
þæt hio leodbealewa   læs gefremede,
inwitniða,   syððan ærest wearð
gyfen goldhroden   geongum cempan,
æðelum diore,   syððan hio Offan flet
1950
ofer fealone flod   be fæder lare
siðe gesohte;   ðær hio syððan well
in gumstole,   gode, mære,
lifgesceafta   lifigende breac,
hiold heahlufan   wið hæleþa brego,
1955
ealles moncynnes   mine gefræge
þone selestan   bi sæm tweonum,

gold and jewels; no journey far
was it thence to go to the giver of rings,
Hygelac Hrethling: at home he dwelt
by the sea-wall close, himself and clan.
1925
Haughty that house, a hero the king,
high the hall, and Hygd {75} right young,
wise and wary, though winters few
in those fortress walls she had found a home,
Haereth's daughter. Nor humble her ways,
1930
nor grudged she gifts to the Geatish men,
of precious treasure. Not Thryth's pride showed she,
folk-queen famed, or that fell deceit.
Was none so daring that durst make bold
(save her lord alone) of the liegemen dear
1935
that lady full in the face to look,
but forged fetters he found his lot,
bonds of death! And brief the respite;
soon as they seized him, his sword-doom was spoken,
and the burnished blade a baleful murder
1940
proclaimed and closed. No queenly way
for woman to practise, though peerless she,
that the weaver-of-peace {76} from warrior dear
by wrath and lying his life should reave!
But Hemming's kinsman hindered this. --
1945
For over their ale men also told
that of these folk-horrors fewer she wrought,
onslaughts of evil, after she went,
gold-decked bride, to the brave young prince,
atheling haughty, and Offa's hall
1950
o'er the fallow flood at her father's bidding
safely sought, where since she prospered,
royal, throned, rich in goods,
fain of the fair life fate had sent her,
and leal in love to the lord of warriors.
1955
He, of all heroes I heard of ever
from sea to sea, of the sons of earth,

eormencynnes.   Forðam Offa wæs
geofum ond guðum,   garcene man,
wide geweorðod,   wisdome heold
1960
eðel sinne;   þonon Eomer woc
hæleðum to helpe,   Hemminges mæg,
nefa Garmundes,   niða cræftig.

most excellent seemed. Hence Offa was praised
for his fighting and feeing by far-off men,
the spear-bold warrior; wisely he ruled
1960
over his empire. Eomer woke to him,
help of heroes, Hemming's kinsman,
Grandson of Garmund, grim in war.

Gewat him ða se hearda   mid his hondscole
sylf æfter sande   sæwong tredan,
1965
wide waroðas.   Woruldcandel scan,
sigel suðan fus.   Hi sið drugon,
elne geeodon,   to ðæs ðe eorla hleo,
bonan Ongenþeoes   burgum in innan,
geongne guðcyning   godne gefrunon
1970
hringas dælan.   Higelace wæs
sið Beowulfes   snude gecyðed,
þæt ðær on worðig   wigendra hleo,
lindgestealla,   lifigende cwom,
heaðolaces hal   to hofe gongan.
1975
Hraðe wæs gerymed,   swa se rica bebead,
feðegestum   flet innanweard.
Gesæt þa wið sylfne   se ða sæcce genæs,
mæg wið mæge,   syððan mandryhten
þurh hleoðorcwyde   holdne gegrette,
1980
meaglum wordum.   Meoduscencum hwearf
geond þæt healreced   Hæreðes dohtor,
lufode ða leode,   liðwæge bær
hæleðum to handa.   Higelac ongan
sinne geseldan   in sele þam hean
1985
fægre fricgcean   (hyne fyrwet bræc,
hwylce Sægeata   siðas wæron):
"Hu lomp eow on lade,   leofa Biowulf,
þa ðu færinga   feorr gehogodest
sæcce secean   ofer sealt wæter,
1990
hilde to Hiorote?   Ac ðu Hroðgare
widcuðne wean   wihte gebettest,
mærum ðeodne?   Ic ðæs modceare
sorhwylmum seað,   siðe ne truwode
leofes mannes;   ic ðe lange bæd
1995
þæt ðu þone wælgæst   wihte ne grette,
lete Suðdene   sylfe geweorðan

XXIX. HIS ARRIVAL. - HYGELAC'S RECEPTION.

HASTENED the hardy one, henchmen with him,
sandy strand of the sea to tread
1965
and widespread ways. The world's great candle,
sun shone from south. They strode along
with sturdy steps to the spot they knew
where the battle-king young, his burg within,
slayer of Ongentheow, shared the rings,
1970
shelter-of-heroes. To Hygelac
Beowulf's coming was quickly told, --
that there in the court the clansmen's refuge,
the shield-companion sound and alive,
hale from the hero-play homeward strode.
1975
With haste in the hall, by highest order,
room for the rovers was readily made.
By his sovran he sat, come safe from battle,
kinsman by kinsman. His kindly lord
he first had greeted in gracious form,
1980
with manly words. The mead dispensing,
came through the high hall Haereth's daughter,
winsome to warriors, wine-cup bore
to the hands of the heroes. Hygelac then
his comrade fairly with question plied
1985
in the lofty hall, sore longing to know
what manner of sojourn the Sea-Geats made.
"What came of thy quest, my kinsman Beowulf,
when thy yearnings suddenly swept thee yonder
battle to seek o'er the briny sea,
1990
combat in Heorot? Hrothgar couldst thou
aid at all, the honored chief,
in his wide-known woes? With waves of care
my sad heart seethed; I sore mistrusted
my loved one's venture: long I begged thee
1995
by no means to seek that slaughtering monster,
but suffer the South-Danes to settle their feud

guðe wið Grendel.   Gode ic þanc secge
þæs ðe ic ðe gesundne   geseon moste."
Biowulf maðelode,   bearn Ecgðioes:
2000
"þæt is undyrne,   dryhten Higelac,
micel gemeting,   monegum fira,
hwylc orleghwil   uncer Grendles
wearð on ðam wange,   þær he worna fela
Sigescyldingum   sorge gefremede,
2005
yrmðe to aldre.   Ic ðæt eall gewræc,
swa begylpan ne þearf   Grendeles maga
ænig ofer eorðan   uhthlem þone,
se ðe lengest leofað   laðan cynnes,
facne bifongen.   Ic ðær furðum cwom
2010
to ðam hringsele   Hroðgar gretan;
sona me se mæra   mago Healfdenes,
syððan he modsefan   minne cuðe,
wið his sylfes sunu   setl getæhte.
Weorod wæs on wynne;   ne seah ic widan feorh
2015
under heofones hwealf   healsittendra
medudream maran.   Hwilum mæru cwen,
friðusibb folca,   flet eall geondhwearf,
bædde byre geonge;   oft hio beahwriðan
secge sealde,   ær hie to setle geong.
2020
Hwilum for duguðe   dohtor Hroðgares
eorlum on ende   ealuwæge bær;
þa ic Freaware   fletsittende
nemnan hyrde,   þær hio nægled sinc
hæleðum sealde.   Sio gehaten is,
2025
geong, goldhroden,   gladum suna Frodan;
hafað þæs geworden   wine Scyldinga,
rices hyrde,   ond þæt ræd talað,
þæt he mid ðy wife   wælfæhða dæl,
sæcca gesette.   Oft seldan hwær
2030
æfter leodhryre   lytle hwile
bongar bugeð,   þeah seo bryd duge!

themselves with Grendel. Now God be thanked
that safe and sound I can see thee now!"
Beowulf spake, the bairn of Ecgtheow: --
2000
"'Tis known and unhidden, Hygelac Lord,
to many men, that meeting of ours,
struggle grim between Grendel and me,
which we fought on the field where full too many
sorrows he wrought for the Scylding-Victors,
2005
evils unending. These all I avenged.
No boast can be from breed of Grendel,
any on earth, for that uproar at dawn,
from the longest-lived of the loathsome race
in fleshly fold! -- But first I went
2010
Hrothgar to greet in the hall of gifts,
where Healfdene's kinsman high-renowned,
soon as my purpose was plain to him,
assigned me a seat by his son and heir.
The liegemen were lusty; my life-days never
2015
such merry men over mead in hall
have I heard under heaven! The high-born queen,
people's peace-bringer, passed through the hall,
cheered the young clansmen, clasps of gold,
ere she sought her seat, to sundry gave.
2020
Oft to the heroes Hrothgar's daughter,
to earls in turn, the ale-cup tendered, --
she whom I heard these hall-companions
Freawaru name, when fretted gold
she proffered the warriors. Promised is she,
2025
gold-decked maid, to the glad son of Froda.
Sage this seems to the Scylding's-friend,
kingdom's-keeper: he counts it wise
the woman to wed so and ward off feud,
store of slaughter. But seldom ever
2030
when men are slain, does the murder-spear sink
but briefest while, though the bride be fair! {77}

Mæg þæs þonne ofþyncan   ðeodne Heaðobeardna
ond þegna gehwam   þara leoda,
þonne he mid fæmnan   on flett gæð,
2035
dryhtbearn Dena,   duguða biwenede;
on him gladiað   gomelra lafe,
heard ond hringmæl   Heaðabeardna gestreon
þenden hie ðam wæpnum   wealdan moston,
oððæt hie forlæddan   to ðam lindplegan
2040
swæse gesiðas   ond hyra sylfra feorh.
þonne cwið æt beore   se ðe beah gesyhð,
eald æscwiga,   se ðe eall geman,
garcwealm gumena   (him bið grim sefa),
onginneð geomormod   geongum cempan
2045
þurh hreðra gehygd   higes cunnian,
wigbealu weccean,   ond þæt word acwyð:
'Meaht ðu, min wine,   mece gecnawan
þone þin fæder   to gefeohte bær
under heregriman   hindeman siðe,
2050
dyre iren,   þær hyne Dene slogon,
weoldon wælstowe,   syððan Wiðergyld læg,
æfter hæleþa hryre,   hwate Scyldungas?
Nu her þara banena   byre nathwylces
frætwum hremig   on flet gæð,
2055
morðres gylpeð,   ond þone maðþum byreð,
þone þe ðu mid rihte   rædan sceoldest.'
Manað swa ond myndgað   mæla gehwylce
sarum wordum,   oððæt sæl cymeð
þæt se fæmnan þegn   fore fæder dædum
2060
æfter billes bite   blodfag swefeð,
ealdres scyldig;   him se oðer þonan
losað lifigende,   con him land geare.
þonne bioð abrocene   on ba healfe
aðsweord eorla;   syððan Ingelde
2065
weallað wælniðas,   ond him wiflufan

XXX. BEOWULF'S STORY OF THE SLAYINGS.

"Nor haply will like it the Heathobard lord,
and as little each of his liegemen all,
when a thane of the Danes, in that doughty throng,
2035
goes with the lady along their hall,
and on him the old-time heirlooms glisten
hard and ring-decked, Heathobard's treasure,
weapons that once they wielded fair
until they lost at the linden-play {78}
2040
liegeman leal and their lives as well.
Then, over the ale, on this heirloom gazing,
some ash-wielder old who has all in mind
that spear-death of men, {79} -- he is stern of mood,
heavy at heart, -- in the hero young
2045
tests the temper and tries the soul
and war-hate wakens, with words like these: --
Canst thou not, comrade, ken that sword
which to the fray thy father carried
in his final feud, 'neath the fighting-mask,
2050
dearest of blades, when the Danish slew him
and wielded the war-place on Withergild's fall,
after havoc of heroes, those hardy Scyldings?
Now, the son of a certain slaughtering Dane,
proud of his treasure, paces this hall,
2055
joys in the killing, and carries the jewel {80}
that rightfully ought to be owned by thee!
Thus he urges and eggs him all the time
with keenest words, till occasion offers
that Freawaru's thane, for his father's deed,
2060
after bite of brand in his blood must slumber,
losing his life; but that liegeman flies
living away, for the land he kens.
And thus be broken on both their sides
oaths of the earls, when Ingeld's breast
2065
wells with war-hate, and wife-love now

æfter cearwælmum colran weorðað.
þy ic Heaðobeardna hyldo ne telge,
dryhtsibbe dæl Denum unfæcne,
freondscipe fæstne. Ic sceal forð sprecan
2070
gen ymbe Grendel, þæt ðu geare cunne,
sinces brytta, to hwan syððan wearð
hondræs hæleða. Syððan heofones gim
glad ofer grundas, gæst yrre cwom,
eatol, æfengrom, user neosan,
2075
ðær we gesunde sæl weardodon.
þær wæs Hondscio hild onsæge,
feorhbealu fægum; he fyrmest læg,
gyrded cempa; him Grendel wearð,
mærum maguþegne to muðbonan,
2080
leofes mannes lic eall forswealg.
No ðy ær ut ða gen idelhende
bona blodigtoð, bealewa gemyndig,
of ðam goldsele gongan wolde,
ac he mægnes rof min costode,
2085
grapode gearofolm. Glof hangode
sid ond syllic, searobendum fæst;
sio wæs orðoncum eall gegyrwed
deofles cræftum ond dracan fellum.
He mec þær on innan unsynnigne,
2090
dior dædfruma, gedon wolde
manigra sumne; hyt ne mihte swa,
syððan ic on yrre uppriht astod.
To lang ys to reccenne hu ic ðam leodsceaðan
yfla gehwylces ondlean forgeald;
2095
þær ic, þeoden min, þine leode
weorðode weorcum. He on weg losade,
lytle hwile lifwynna breac;
hwæþre him sio swiðre swaðe weardade
hand on Hiorte, ond he hean ðonan
2100
modes geomor meregrund gefeoll.
Me þone wælræs wine Scildunga

after the care-billows cooler grows.
"So {81} I hold not high the Heathobards' faith
due to the Danes, or their during love
and pact of peace. -- But I pass from that,
2070
turning to Grendel, O giver-of-treasure,
and saying in full how the fight resulted,
hand-fray of heroes. When heaven's jewel
had fled o'er far fields, that fierce sprite came,
night-foe savage, to seek us out
2075
where safe and sound we sentried the hall.
To Hondscio then was that harassing deadly,
his fall there was fated. He first was slain,
girded warrior. Grendel on him
turned murderous mouth, on our mighty kinsman,
2080
and all of the brave man's body devoured.
Yet none the earlier, empty-handed,
would the bloody-toothed murderer, mindful of bale,
outward go from the gold-decked hall:
but me he attacked in his terror of might,
2085
with greedy hand grasped me. A glove hung by him {82}
wide and wondrous, wound with bands;
and in artful wise it all was wrought,
by devilish craft, of dragon-skins.
Me therein, an innocent man,
2090
the fiendish foe was fain to thrust
with many another. He might not so,
when I all angrily upright stood.
'Twere long to relate how that land-destroyer
I paid in kind for his cruel deeds;
2095
yet there, my prince, this people of thine
got fame by my fighting. He fled away,
and a little space his life preserved;
but there staid behind him his stronger hand
left in Heorot; heartsick thence
2100
on the floor of the ocean that outcast fell.
Me for this struggle the Scyldings'-friend

fættan golde fela leanode,
manegum maðmum, syððan mergen com
ond we to symble geseten hæfdon.
2105
þær wæs gidd ond gleo. Gomela Scilding,
felafricgende, feorran rehte;
hwilum hildedeor hearpan wynne,
gomenwudu grette, hwilum gyd awræc
soð ond sarlic, hwilum syllic spell
2110
rehte æfter rihte rumheort cyning.
Hwilum eft ongan, eldo gebunden,
gomel guðwiga gioguðe cwiðan,
hildestrengo; hreðer inne weoll,
þonne he wintrum frod worn gemunde.
2115
Swa we þær inne ondlangne dæg
niode naman, oððæt niht becwom
oðer to yldum. þa wæs eft hraðe
gearo gyrnwræce Grendeles modor,
siðode sorhfull; sunu deað fornam,
2120
wighete Wedra. Wif unhyre
hyre bearn gewræc, beorn acwealde
ellenlice; þær wæs æschere,
frodan fyrnwitan, feorh uðgenge.
Noðer hy hine ne moston, syððan mergen cwom,
2125
deaðwerigne, Denia leode,
bronde forbærnan, ne on bæl hladan
leofne mannan; hio þæt lic ætbær
feondes fæðmum under firgenstream.
þæt wæs Hroðgare hreowa tornost
2130
þara þe leodfruman lange begeate.
þa se ðeoden mec ðine life
healsode hreohmod, þæt ic on holma geþring
eorlscipe efnde, ealdre geneðde,
mærðo fremede; he me mede gehet.
2135
Ic ða ðæs wælmes, þe is wide cuð,
grimne gryrelicne grundhyrde fond;
þær unc hwile wæs hand gemæne,

paid in plenty with plates of gold,
with many a treasure, when morn had come
and we all at the banquet-board sat down.
2105
Then was song and glee. The gray-haired Scylding,
much tested, told of the times of yore.
Whiles the hero his harp bestirred,
wood-of-delight; now lays he chanted
of sooth and sadness, or said aright
2110
legends of wonder, the wide-hearted king;
or for years of his youth he would yearn at times,
for strength of old struggles, now stricken with age,
hoary hero: his heart surged full
when, wise with winters, he wailed their flight.
2115
Thus in the hall the whole of that day
at ease we feasted, till fell o'er earth
another night. Anon full ready
in greed of vengeance, Grendel's mother
set forth all doleful. Dead was her son
2120
through war-hate of Weders; now, woman monstrous
with fury fell a foeman she slew,
avenged her offspring. From Aeschere old,
loyal councillor, life was gone;
nor might they e'en, when morning broke,
2125
those Danish people, their death-done comrade
burn with brands, on balefire lay
the man they mourned. Under mountain stream
she had carried the corpse with cruel hands.
For Hrothgar that was the heaviest sorrow
2130
of all that had laden the lord of his folk.
The leader then, by thy life, besought me
(sad was his soul) in the sea-waves' coil
to play the hero and hazard my being
for glory of prowess: my guerdon he pledged.
2135
I then in the waters -- 'tis widely known --
that sea-floor-guardian savage found.
Hand-to-hand there a while we struggled;

holm heolfre weoll,   ond ic heafde becearf
in ðam guðsele   Grendeles modor
2140
eacnum ecgum,   unsofte þonan
feorh oðferede.   Næs ic fæge þa gyt,
ac me eorla hleo   eft gesealde
maðma menigeo,   maga Healfdenes.

billows welled blood; in the briny hall
her head I hewed with a hardy blade
2140
from Grendel's mother, -- and gained my life,
though not without danger. My doom was not yet.
Then the haven-of-heroes, Healfdene's son,
gave me in guerdon great gifts of price.

Swa se ðeodkyning   þeawum lyfde.
2145
Nealles ic ðam leanum   forloren hæfde,
mægnes mede,   ac he me maðmas geaf,
sunu Healfdenes,   on minne sylfes dom;
ða ic ðe, beorncyning,   bringan wylle,
estum geywan.   Gen is eall æt ðe
2150
lissa gelong;   ic lyt hafo
heafodmaga   nefne, Hygelac, ðec."
Het ða in beran   eaforheafodsegn,
heaðosteapne helm,   hare byrnan,
guðsweord geatolic,   gyd æfter wræc:
2155
"Me ðis hildesceorp   Hroðgar sealde,
snotra fengel,   sume worde het
þæt ic his ærest ðe   est gesægde;
cwæð þæt hyt hæfde   Hiorogar cyning,
leod Scyldunga   lange hwile;
2160
no ðy ær suna sinum   syllan wolde,
hwatum Heorowearde,   þeah he him hold wære,
breostgewædu.   Bruc ealles well!"
Hyrde ic þæt þam frætwum   feower mearas
lungre, gelice,   last weardode,
2165
æppelfealuwe;   he him est geteah
meara ond maðma.   Swa sceal mæg don,
nealles inwitnet   oðrum bregdon
dyrnum cræfte,   deað renian
hondgesteallan.   Hygelace wæs,
2170
niða heardum,   nefa swyðe hold,
ond gehwæðer oðrum   hroþra gemyndig.
Hyrde ic þæt he ðone healsbeah   Hygde gesealde,
wrætlicne wundurmaððum,   ðone þe him Wealhðeo
geaf,
ðeodnes dohtor,   þrio wicg somod

XXXI. HE GIVES PRESENTS TO HYGELAC.
-HYGELAC REWARDS HIM.
-HYGELAC'S DEATH.
-BEOWULF REIGNS.

"So held this king to the customs old,
2145
that I wanted for nought in the wage I gained,
the meed of my might; he made me gifts,
Healfdene's heir, for my own disposal.
Now to thee, my prince, I proffer them all,
gladly give them. Thy grace alone
2150
can find me favor. Few indeed
have I of kinsmen, save, Hygelac, thee!"
Then he bade them bear him the boar-head standard,
the battle-helm high, and breastplate gray,
the splendid sword; then spake in form: --
2155
"Me this war-gear the wise old prince,
Hrothgar, gave, and his hest he added,
that its story be straightway said to thee. --
A while it was held by Heorogar king,
for long time lord of the land of Scyldings;
2160
yet not to his son the sovran left it,
to daring Heoroweard, -- dear as he was to him,
his harness of battle. -- Well hold thou it all!"
And I heard that soon passed o'er the path of this treasure,
all apple-fallow, four good steeds,
2165
each like the others, arms and horses
he gave to the king. So should kinsmen be,
not weave one another the net of wiles,
or with deep-hid treachery death contrive
for neighbor and comrade. His nephew was ever
2170
by hardy Hygelac held full dear,
and each kept watch o'er the other's weal.
I heard, too, the necklace to Hygd he presented,
wonder-wrought treasure, which Wealhtheow gave him
sovran's daughter: three steeds he added,

2175
swancor ond sadolbeorht;   hyre syððan wæs
æfter beahðege   breost geweorðod.
Swa bealdode   bearn Ecgðeowes,
guma guðum cuð,   godum dædum,
dreah æfter dome,   nealles druncne slog
2180
heorðgeneatas;   næs him hreoh sefa,
ac he mancynnes   mæste cræfte
ginfæstan gife,   þe him god sealde,
heold hildedeor.   Hean wæs lange,
swa hyne Geata bearn   godne ne tealdon,
2185
ne hyne on medobence   micles wyrðne
drihten Wedera   gedon wolde;
swyðe wendon   þæt he sleac wære,
æðeling unfrom.   Edwenden cwom
tireadigum menn   torna gehwylces.
2190
Het ða eorla hleo   in gefetian,
heaðorof cyning,   Hreðles lafe
golde gegyrede;   næs mid Geatum ða
sincmaðþum selra   on sweordes had;
þæt he on Biowulfes   bearm alegde
2195
ond him gesealde   seofan þusendo,
bold ond bregostol.   Him wæs bam samod
on ðam leodscipe   lond gecynde,
eard, eðelriht,   oðrum swiðor
side rice   þam ðær selra wæs.
2200
Eft þæt geiode   ufaran dogrum
hildehlæmmum,   syððan Hygelac læg
ond Heardrede   hildemeceas
under bordhreoðan   to bonan wurdon,
ða hyne gesohtan   on sigeþeode
2205
hearde hildefrecan,   Heaðoscilfingas,
niða genægdan   nefan Hererices,
syððan Beowulfe   brade rice
on hand gehwearf;   he geheold tela
fiftig wintra   (wæs ða frod cyning,

2175
slender and saddle-gay. Since such gift
the gem gleamed bright on the breast of the queen.
Thus showed his strain the son of Ecgtheow
as a man remarked for mighty deeds
and acts of honor. At ale he slew not
2180
comrade or kin; nor cruel his mood,
though of sons of earth his strength was greatest,
a glorious gift that God had sent
the splendid leader. Long was he spurned,
and worthless by Geatish warriors held;
2185
him at mead the master-of-clans
failed full oft to favor at all.
Slack and shiftless the strong men deemed him,
profitless prince; but payment came,
to the warrior honored, for all his woes. --
2190
Then the bulwark-of-earls {83} bade bring within,
hardy chieftain, Hrethel's heirloom
garnished with gold: no Geat e'er knew
in shape of a sword a statelier prize.
The brand he laid in Beowulf's lap;
2195
and of hides assigned him seven thousand, {84}
with house and high-seat. They held in common
land alike by their line of birth,
inheritance, home: but higher the king
because of his rule o'er the realm itself.
2200
Now further it fell with the flight of years,
with harryings horrid, that Hygelac perished, {85}
and Heardred, too, by hewing of swords
under the shield-wall slaughtered lay,
when him at the van of his victor-folk
2205
sought hardy heroes, Heatho-Scilfings,
in arms o'erwhelming Hereric's nephew.
Then Beowulf came as king this broad
realm to wield; and he ruled it well
fifty winters, {86} a wise old prince,

2210
eald eþelweard),   oððæt an ongan
deorcum nihtum   draca ricsian,
se ðe on heaum hofe   hord beweotode,
stanbeorh steapne;   stig under læg,
eldum uncuð.   þær on innan giong
2215
niða nathwylc,   se ðe neh gefeng
hæðnum horde,   hond ......,
since fahne.   He þæt syððan ......,
þeah ðe he slæpende   besyred wurde
þeofes cræfte;   þæt sie ðiod onfand,
2220
bufolc beorna,   þæt he gebolgen wæs.

2210
warding his land, until One began
in the dark of night, a Dragon, to rage.
In the grave on the hill a hoard it guarded,
in the stone-barrow steep. A strait path reached it,
unknown to mortals. Some man, however,
2215
came by chance that cave within
to the heathen hoard. {87} In hand he took
a golden goblet, nor gave he it back,
stole with it away, while the watcher slept,
by thievish wiles: for the warden's wrath
2220
prince and people must pay betimes!

Nealles mid gewealdum   wyrmhord abræc
sylfes willum,   se ðe him sare gesceod,
ac for þreanedlan   þeow nathwylces
hæleða bearna   heteswengeas fleah,
2225
ærnes þearfa,   ond ðær inne fealh,
secg synbysig,   sona onfunde
þæt þær ðam gyste   gryrebroga stod;
hwæðre earmsceapen
...sceapen
2230
    þa hyne se fær begeat.
Sincfæt ......;   þær wæs swylcra fela
in ðam eorðhuse   ærgestreona,
swa hy on geardagum   gumena nathwylc,
eormenlafe   æþelan cynnes,
2235
þanchycgende   þær gehydde,
deore maðmas.   Ealle hie deað fornam
ærran mælum,   ond se an ða gen
leoda duguðe,   se ðær lengest hwearf,
weard winegeomor,   wende þæs ylcan,
2240
þæt he lytel fæc   longgestreona
brucan moste.   Beorh eallgearo
wunode on wonge   wæteryðum neah,
niwe be næsse,   nearocræftum fæst.
þær on innan bær   eorlgestreona
2245
hringa hyrde   hordwyrðne dæl,
fættan goldes,   fea worda cwæð:
"Heald þu nu, hruse,   nu hæleð ne moston, .
eorla æhte!   Hwæt, hyt ær on ðe
gode begeaton.   Guðdeað fornam,
2250
feorhbealo frecne,   fyra gehwylcne
leoda minra,   þara ðe þis lif ofgeaf,
gesawon seledream.   Ic nah hwa sweord wege
oððe feormie   fæted wæge,
dryncfæt deore;   duguð ellor sceoc.

XXXII. THE FIRE-DRAKE. -THE HOARD.

THAT way he went with no will of his own,
in danger of life, to the dragon's hoard,
but for pressure of peril, some prince's thane.
He fled in fear the fatal scourge,
2225
seeking shelter, a sinful man,
and entered in. At the awful sight
tottered that guest, and terror seized him;
yet the wretched fugitive rallied anon
from fright and fear ere he fled away,
2230
and took the cup from that treasure-hoard.
Of such besides there was store enough,
heirlooms old, the earth below,
which some earl forgotten, in ancient years,
left the last of his lofty race,
2235
heedfully there had hidden away,
dearest treasure. For death of yore
had hurried all hence; and he alone
left to live, the last of the clan,
weeping his friends, yet wished to bide
2240
warding the treasure, his one delight,
though brief his respite. The barrow, new-ready,
to strand and sea-waves stood anear,
hard by the headland, hidden and closed;
there laid within it his lordly heirlooms
2245
and heaped hoard of heavy gold
that warden of rings. Few words he spake:
"Now hold thou, earth, since heroes may not,
what earls have owned! Lo, erst from thee
brave men brought it! But battle-death seized
2250
and cruel killing my clansmen all,
robbed them of life and a liegeman's joys.
None have I left to lift the sword,
or to cleanse the carven cup of price,
beaker bright. My brave are gone.

2255
Sceal se hearda helm   hyrsted golde
fætum befeallen;   feormynd swefað,
þa ðe beadogriman   bywan sceoldon,
ge swylce seo herepad,   sio æt hilde gebad
ofer borda gebræc   bite irena,
2260
brosnað æfter beorne.   Ne mæg byrnan hring
æfter wigfruman   wide feran,
hæleðum be healfe.   Næs hearpan wyn,
gomen gleobeames,   ne god hafoc
geond sæl swingeð,   ne se swifta mearh
2265
burhstede beateð.   Bealocwealm hafað
fela feorhcynna   forð onsended!"
Swa giomormod   giohðo mænde
an æfter eallum,   unbliðe hwearf
dæges ond nihtes,   oððæt deaðes wylm
2270
hran æt heortan.   Hordwynne fond
eald uhtsceaða   opene standan,
se ðe byrnende   biorgas seceð,
nacod niðdraca,   nihtes fleogeð
fyre befangen;   hyne foldbuend
2275
swiðe ondrædað.   He gesecean sceall
hord on hrusan,   þær he hæðen gold
warað wintrum frod,   ne byð him wihte ðy sel.
Swa se ðeodsceaða   þreo hund wintra
heold on hrusan   hordærna sum,
2280
eacencræftig,   oððæt hyne an abealch
mon on mode;   mandryhtne bær
fæted wæge,   frioðowære bæd
hlaford sinne.   ða wæs hord rasod,
onboren beaga hord,   bene getiðad
2285
feasceaftum men.   Frea sceawode
fira fyrngeweorc   forman siðe.
þa se wyrm onwoc,   wroht wæs geniwad;
stonc ða æfter stane,   stearcheort onfand
feondes fotlast;   he to forð gestop
2290

2255
And the helmet hard, all haughty with gold,
shall part from its plating. Polishers sleep
who could brighten and burnish the battle-mask;
and those weeds of war that were wont to brave
over bicker of shields the bite of steel
2260
rust with their bearer. The ringed mail
fares not far with famous chieftain,
at side of hero! No harp's delight,
no glee-wood's gladness! No good hawk now
flies through the hall! Nor horses fleet
2265
stamp in the burgstead! Battle and death
the flower of my race have reft away."
Mournful of mood, thus he moaned his woe,
alone, for them all, and unblithe wept
by day and by night, till death's fell wave
2270
o'erwhelmed his heart. His hoard-of-bliss
that old ill-doer open found,
who, blazing at twilight the barrows haunteth,
naked foe-dragon flying by night
folded in fire: the folk of earth
2275
dread him sore. 'Tis his doom to seek
hoard in the graves, and heathen gold
to watch, many-wintered: nor wins he thereby!
Powerful this plague-of-the-people thus
held the house of the hoard in earth
2280
three hundred winters; till One aroused
wrath in his breast, to the ruler bearing
that costly cup, and the king implored
for bond of peace. So the barrow was plundered,
borne off was booty. His boon was granted
2285
that wretched man; and his ruler saw
first time what was fashioned in far-off days.
When the dragon awoke, new woe was kindled.
O'er the stone he snuffed. The stark-heart found
footprint of foe who so far had gone

2290
dyrnan cræfte   dracan heafde neah.
Swa mæg unfæge   eaðe gedigan
wean ond wræcsið,   se ðe waldendes
hyldo gehealdeþ!   Hordweard sohte
georne æfter grunde,   wolde guman findan,
2295
þone þe him on sweofote   sare geteode,
hat ond hreohmod   hlæw oft ymbehwearf
ealne utanweardne,   ne ðær ænig mon
on þære westenne;   hwæðre wiges gefeh,
beaduwe weorces,   hwilum on beorh æthwearf,
2300
sincfæt sohte.   He þæt sona onfand
ðæt hæfde gumena sum   goldes gefandod,
heahgestreona.   Hordweard onbad
earfoðlice   oððæt æfen cwom;
wæs ða gebolgen   beorges hyrde,
2305
wolde se laða   lige forgyldan
drincfæt dyre.   þa wæs dæg sceacen
wyrme on willan;   no on wealle læg,
bidan wolde,   ac mid bæle for,
fyre gefysed.   Wæs se fruma egeslic
2310
leodum on lande,   swa hyt lungre wearð
on hyra sincgifan   sare geendod.

2290
in his hidden craft by the creature's head. --
So may the undoomed easily flee
evils and exile, if only he gain
the grace of The Wielder! -- That warden of gold
o'er the ground went seeking, greedy to find
2295
the man who wrought him such wrong in sleep.
Savage and burning, the barrow he circled
all without; nor was any there,
none in the waste.... Yet war he desired,
was eager for battle. The barrow he entered,
2300
sought the cup, and discovered soon
that some one of mortals had searched his treasure,
his lordly gold. The guardian waited
ill-enduring till evening came;
boiling with wrath was the barrow's keeper,
2305
and fain with flame the foe to pay
for the dear cup's loss. -- Now day was fled
as the worm had wished. By its wall no more
was it glad to bide, but burning flew
folded in flame: a fearful beginning
2310
for sons of the soil; and soon it came,
in the doom of their lord, to a dreadful end.

Ða se gæst ongan   gledum spiwan,
beorht hofu bærnan;   bryneleoma stod
eldum on andan.   No ðær aht cwices
2315
lað lyftfloga   læfan wolde.
Wæs þæs wyrmes wig   wide gesyne,
nearofages nið   nean ond feorran,
hu se guðsceaða   Geata leode
hatode ond hynde;   hord eft gesceat,
2320
dryhtsele dyrnne,   ær dæges hwile.
Hæfde landwara   lige befangen,
bæle ond bronde,   beorges getruwode,
wiges ond wealles;   him seo wen geleah.
þa wæs Biowulfe   broga gecyðed
2325
snude to soðe,   þæt his sylfes ham,
bolda selest,   brynewylmum mealt,
gifstol Geata.   þæt ðam godan wæs
hreow on hreðre,   hygesorga mæst;
wende se wisa   þæt he wealdende
2330
ofer ealde riht,   ecean dryhtne,
bitre gebulge.   Breost innan weoll
þeostrum geþoncum,   swa him geþywe ne wæs.
Hæfde ligdraca   leoda fæsten,
ealond utan,   eorðweard ðone
2335
gledum forgrunden;   him ðæs guðkyning,
Wedera þioden,   wræce leornode.
Heht him þa gewyrcean   wigendra hleo
eallirenne,   eorla dryhten,
wigbord wrætlic;   wisse he gearwe
2340
þæt him holtwudu   helpan ne meahte,
lind wið lige.   Sceolde lændaga
æþeling ærgod   ende gebidan,
worulde lifes,   ond se wyrm somod,
þeah ðe hordwelan   heolde lange.

XXXIII. BEOWULF RESOLVES TO KILL THE FIRE-DRAKE.

THEN the baleful fiend its fire belched out,
and bright homes burned. The blaze stood high
all landsfolk frighting. No living thing
2315
would that loathly one leave as aloft it flew.
Wide was the dragon's warring seen,
its fiendish fury far and near,
as the grim destroyer those Geatish people
hated and hounded. To hidden lair,
2320
to its hoard it hastened at hint of dawn.
Folk of the land it had lapped in flame,
with bale and brand. In its barrow it trusted,
its battling and bulwarks: that boast was vain!
To Beowulf then the bale was told
2325
quickly and truly: the king's own home,
of buildings the best, in brand-waves melted,
that gift-throne of Geats. To the good old man
sad in heart, 'twas heaviest sorrow.
The sage assumed that his sovran God
2330
he had angered, breaking ancient law,
and embittered the Lord. His breast within
with black thoughts welled, as his wont was never.
The folk's own fastness that fiery dragon
with flame had destroyed, and the stronghold all
2335
washed by waves; but the warlike king,
prince of the Weders, plotted vengeance.
Warriors'-bulwark, he bade them work
all of iron -- the earl's commander --
a war-shield wondrous: well he knew
2340
that forest-wood against fire were worthless,
linden could aid not. -- Atheling brave,
he was fated to finish this fleeting life, {88}
his days on earth, and the dragon with him,
though long it had watched o'er the wealth of the hoard! -
-

2345
Oferhogode ða   hringa fengel
þæt he þone widflogan   weorode gesohte,
sidan herge;   no he him þa sæcce ondred,
ne him þæs wyrmes wig   for wiht dyde,
eafoð ond ellen,   forðon he ær fela
2350
nearo neðende   niða gedigde,
hildehlemma,   syððan he Hroðgares,
sigoreadig secg,   sele fælsode
ond æt guðe forgrap   Grendeles mægum
laðan cynnes.   No þæt læsest wæs
2355
hondgemota,   þær mon Hygelac sloh,
syððan Geata cyning   guðe ræsum,
freawine folca   Freslondum on,
Hreðles eafora   hiorodryncum swealt,
bille gebeaten.   þonan Biowulf com
2360
sylfes cræfte,   sundnytte dreah;
hæfde him on earme   ana *XXX*
hildegeatwa,   þa he to holme beag.
Nealles Hetware   hremge þorfton
feðewiges,   þe him foran ongean
2365
linde bæron;   lyt eft becwom
fram þam hildfrecan   hames niosan.
Oferswam ða sioleða bigong   sunu Ecgðeowes,
earm anhaga,   eft to leodum;
þær him Hygd gebead   hord ond rice,
2370
beagas ond bregostol,   bearne ne truwode
þæt he wið ælfylcum   eþelstolas
healdan cuðe,   ða wæs Hygelac dead.
No ðy ær feasceafte   findan meahton
æt ðam æðelinge   ænige ðinga,
2375
þæt he Heardrede   hlaford wære
oððe þone cynedom   ciosan wolde;
hwæðre he him on folce   freondlarum heold,
estum mid are,   oððæt he yldra wearð,
Wedergeatum weold.   Hyne wræcmæcgas

2345
Shame he reckoned it, sharer-of-rings,
to follow the flyer-afar with a host,
a broad-flung band; nor the battle feared he,
nor deemed he dreadful the dragon's warring,
its vigor and valor: ventures desperate
2350
he had passed a-plenty, and perils of war,
contest-crash, since, conqueror proud,
Hrothgar's hall he had wholly purged,
and in grapple had killed the kin of Grendel,
loathsome breed! Not least was that
2355
of hand-to-hand fights where Hygelac fell,
when the ruler of Geats in rush of battle,
lord of his folk, in the Frisian land,
son of Hrethel, by sword-draughts died,
by brands down-beaten. Thence Beowulf fled
2360
through strength of himself and his swimming power,
though alone, and his arms were laden with thirty
coats of mail, when he came to the sea!
Nor yet might Hetwaras {89} haughtily boast
their craft of contest, who carried against him
2365
shields to the fight: but few escaped
from strife with the hero to seek their homes!
Then swam over ocean Ecgtheow's son
lonely and sorrowful, seeking his land,
where Hygd made him offer of hoard and realm,
2370
rings and royal-seat, reckoning naught
the strength of her son to save their kingdom
from hostile hordes, after Hygelac's death.
No sooner for this could the stricken ones
in any wise move that atheling's mind
2375
over young Heardred's head as lord
and ruler of all the realm to be:
yet the hero upheld him with helpful words,
aided in honor, till, older grown,
he wielded the Weder-Geats. -- Wandering exiles

2380
ofer sæ sohtan,   suna Ohteres;
hæfdon hy forhealden   helm Scylfinga,
þone selestan   sæcyninga
þara ðe in Swiorice   sinc brytnade,
mærne þeoden.   Him þæt to mearce wearð;
2385
he þær for feorme   feorhwunde hleat
sweordes swengum,   sunu Hygelaces,
ond him eft gewat   Ongenðioes bearn
hames niosan,   syððan Heardred læg,
let ðone bregostol   Biowulf healdan,
2390
Geatum wealdan.   þæt wæs god cyning!

2380
sought him o'er seas, the sons of Ohtere,
who had spurned the sway of the Scylfings'-helmet,
the bravest and best that broke the rings,
in Swedish land, of the sea-kings' line,
haughty hero. {90} Hence Heardred's end.
2385
For shelter he gave them, sword-death came,
the blade's fell blow, to bairn of Hygelac;
but the son of Ongentheow sought again
house and home when Heardred fell,
leaving Beowulf lord of Geats
2390
and gift-seat's master. -- A good king he!

Se ðæs leodhryres   lean gemunde
uferan dogrum,   Eadgilse wearð
feasceaftum freond,   folce gestepte
ofer sæ side   sunu Ohteres,
2395
wigum ond wæpnum;   he gewræc syððan
cealdum cearsiðum,   cyning ealdre bineat.
Swa he niða gehwane   genesen hæfde,
sliðra geslyhta,   sunu Ecgðiowes,
ellenweorca,   oð ðone anne dæg
2400
þe he wið þam wyrme   gewegan sceolde.
Gewat þa XIIa sum   torne gebolgen
dryhten Geata   dracan sceawian.
Hæfde þa gefrunen   hwanan sio fæhð aras,
bealonið biorna;   him to bearme cwom
2405
maðþumfæt mære   þurh ðæs meldan hond.
Se wæs on ðam ðreate   þreotteoða secg,
se ðæs orleges   or onstealde,
hæft hygegiomor,   sceolde hean ðonon
wong wisian.   He ofer willan giong
2410
to ðæs ðe he eorðsele   anne wisse,
hlæw under hrusan   holmwylme neh,
yðgewinne;   se wæs innan full
wrætta ond wira.   Weard unhiore,
gearo guðfreca,   goldmaðmas heold,
2415
eald under eorðan.   Næs þæt yðe ceap
to gegangenne   gumena ænigum!
Gesæt ða on næsse   niðheard cyning,
þenden hælo abead   heorðgeneatum,
goldwine Geata.   Him wæs geomor sefa,
2420
wæfre ond wælfus,   wyrd ungemete neah,
se ðone gomelan   gretan sceolde,
secean sawle hord,   sundur gedælan
lif wið lice,   no þon lange wæs
feorh æþelinges   flæsce bewunden.

XXXIV. RETROSPECT OF BEOWULF.
-STRIFE BETWEEN SWEONAS AND GEATAS.

THE fall of his lord he was fain to requite
in after days; and to Eadgils he proved
friend to the friendless, and forces sent
over the sea to the son of Ohtere,
2395
weapons and warriors: well repaid he
those care-paths cold when the king he slew. {91}
Thus safe through struggles the son of Ecgtheow
had passed a plenty, through perils dire,
with daring deeds, till this day was come
2400
that doomed him now with the dragon to strive.
With comrades eleven the lord of Geats
swollen in rage went seeking the dragon.
He had heard whence all the harm arose
and the killing of clansmen; that cup of price
2405
on the lap of the lord had been laid by the finder.
In the throng was this one thirteenth man,
starter of all the strife and ill,
care-laden captive; cringing thence
forced and reluctant, he led them on
2410
till he came in ken of that cavern-hall,
the barrow delved near billowy surges,
flood of ocean. Within 'twas full
of wire-gold and jewels; a jealous warden,
warrior trusty, the treasures held,
2415
lurked in his lair. Not light the task
of entrance for any of earth-born men!
Sat on the headland the hero king,
spake words of hail to his hearth-companions,
gold-friend of Geats. All gloomy his soul,
2420
wavering, death-bound. Wyrd full nigh
stood ready to greet the gray-haired man,
to seize his soul-hoard, sunder apart
life and body. Not long would be
the warrior's spirit enwound with flesh.

2425
Biowulf maþelade,   bearn Ecgðeowes:
"Fela ic on giogoðe   guðræsa genæs,
orleghwila;   ic þæt eall gemon.
Ic wæs syfanwintre,   þa mec sinca baldor,
freawine folca,   æt minum fæder genam;
2430
heold mec ond hæfde   Hreðel cyning,
geaf me sinc ond symbel,   sibbe gemunde.
Næs ic him to life   laðra owihte,
beorn in burgum,   þonne his bearna hwylc,
Herebeald ond Hæðcyn   oððe Hygelac min.
2435
Wæs þam yldestan   ungedefelice
mæges dædum   morþorbed stred,
syððan hyne Hæðcyn   of hornbogan,
his freawine,   flane geswencte,
miste mercelses   ond his mæg ofscet,
2440
broðor oðerne   blodigan gare.
þæt wæs feohleas gefeoht,   fyrenum gesyngad,
hreðre hygemeðe;   sceolde hwæðre swa þeah
æðeling unwrecen   ealdres linnan.
Swa bið geomorlic   gomelum ceorle
2445
to gebidanne,   þæt his byre ride
giong on galgan,   þonne he gyd wrece,
sarigne sang,   þonne his sunu hangað
hrefne to hroðre,   ond he him helpe ne mæg,
eald ond infrod,   ænige gefremman.
2450
Symble bið gemyndgad   morna gehwylce
eaforan ellorsið;   oðres ne gymeð
to gebidanne   burgum in innan
yrfeweardas,   þonne se an hafað
þurh deaðes nyd   dæda gefondad.
2455
Gesyhð sorhcearig   on his suna bure
winsele westne,   windge reste
reote berofene.   Ridend swefað,
hæleð in hoðman;   nis þær hearpan sweg,
gomen in geardum,   swylce ðær iu wæron.

180

2425
Beowulf spake, the bairn of Ecgtheow: --
"Through store of struggles I strove in youth,
mighty feuds; I mind them all.
I was seven years old when the sovran of rings,
friend-of-his-folk, from my father took me,
2430
had me, and held me, Hrethel the king,
with food and fee, faithful in kinship.
Ne'er, while I lived there, he loathlier found me,
bairn in the burg, than his birthright sons,
Herebeald and Haethcyn and Hygelac mine.
2435
For the eldest of these, by unmeet chance,
by kinsman's deed, was the death-bed strewn,
when Haethcyn killed him with horny bow,
his own dear liege laid low with an arrow,
missed the mark and his mate shot down,
2440
one brother the other, with bloody shaft.
A feeless fight, {92} and a fearful sin,
horror to Hrethel; yet, hard as it was,
unavenged must the atheling die!
Too awful it is for an aged man
2445
to bide and bear, that his bairn so young
rides on the gallows. A rime he makes,
sorrow-song for his son there hanging
as rapture of ravens; no rescue now
can come from the old, disabled man!
2450
Still is he minded, as morning breaks,
of the heir gone elsewhere; {93} another he hopes not
he will bide to see his burg within
as ward for his wealth, now the one has found
doom of death that the deed incurred.
2455
Forlorn he looks on the lodge of his son,
wine-hall waste and wind-swept chambers
reft of revel. The rider sleepeth,
the hero, far-hidden; {94} no harp resounds,
in the courts no wassail, as once was heard.

2460
Gewiteð þonne on sealman,   sorhleoð gæleð
an æfter anum;   þuhte him eall to rum,
wongas ond wicstede.   Swa Wedra helm
æfter Herebealde   heortan sorge
weallende wæg.   Wihte ne meahte
2465
on ðam feorhbonan   fæghðe gebetan;
no ðy ær he þone heaðorinc   hatian ne meahte
laðum dædum,   þeah him leof ne wæs.
He ða mid þære sorhge,   þe him swa sar belamp,
gumdream ofgeaf,   godes leoht geceas,
2470
eaferum læfde,   swa deð eadig mon,
lond ond leodbyrig,   þa he of life gewat.
þa wæs synn ond sacu   Sweona ond Geata
ofer wid wæter,   wroht gemæne,
herenið hearda,   syððan Hreðel swealt,
2475
oððe him Ongenðeowes   eaferan wæran
frome, fyrdhwate,   freode ne woldon
ofer heafo healdan,   ac ymb Hreosnabeorh
eatolne inwitscear   oft gefremedon.
þæt mægwine   mine gewræcan,
2480
fæhðe ond fyrene,   swa hyt gefræge wæs,
þeah ðe oðer his   ealdre gebohte,
heardan ceape;   Hæðcynne wearð,
Geata dryhtne,   guð onsæge.
þa ic on morgne gefrægn   mæg oðerne
2485
billes ecgum   on bonan stælan,
þær Ongenþeow   Eofores niosað.
Guðhelm toglad,   gomela Scylfing
hreas hildeblac;   hond gemunde
fæhðo genoge,   feorhsweng ne ofteah.
2490
Ic him þa maðmas,   þe he me sealde,
geald æt guðe,   swa me gifeðe wæs,
leohtan sweorde;   he me lond forgeaf,

XXXV. MEMORIES OF PAST TIME.
-THE FEUD WITH THE FIRE-DRAKE.

2460
"THEN he goes to his chamber, a grief-song chants
alone for his lost. Too large all seems,
homestead and house. So the helmet-of-Weders
hid in his heart for Herebeald
waves of woe. No way could he take
2465
to avenge on the slayer slaughter so foul;
nor e'en could he harass that hero at all
with loathing deed, though he loved him not.
And so for the sorrow his soul endured,
men's gladness he gave up and God's light chose.
2470
Lands and cities he left his sons
(as the wealthy do) when he went from earth.
There was strife and struggle 'twixt Swede and Geat
o'er the width of waters; war arose,
hard battle-horror, when Hrethel died,
2475
and Ongentheow's offspring grew
strife-keen, bold, nor brooked o'er the seas
pact of peace, but pushed their hosts
to harass in hatred by Hreosnabeorh.
Men of my folk for that feud had vengeance,
2480
for woful war ('tis widely known),
though one of them bought it with blood of his heart,
a bargain hard: for Haethcyn proved
fatal that fray, for the first-of-Geats.
At morn, I heard, was the murderer killed
2485
by kinsman for kinsman, {95} with clash of sword,
when Ongentheow met Eofor there.
Wide split the war-helm: wan he fell,
hoary Scylfing; the hand that smote him
of feud was mindful, nor flinched from the death-blow.
2490
-- "For all that he {96} gave me, my gleaming sword
repaid him at war, -- such power I wielded, --
for lordly treasure: with land he entrusted me,

eard, eðelwyn.   Næs him ænig þearf
þæt he to Gifðum   oððe to Gardenum
2495
oððe in Swiorice   secean þurfe
wyrsan wigfrecan,   weorðe gecypan.
Symle ic him on feðan   beforan wolde,
ana on orde,   ond swa to aldre sceall
sæcce fremman,   þenden þis sweord þolað,
2500
þæt mec ær ond sið   oft gelæste.
Syððan ic for dugeðum   Dæghrefne wearð
to handbonan,   Huga cempan;
nalles he ða frætwe   Frescyninge,
breostweorðunge,   bringan moste,
2505
ac in compe gecrong   cumbles hyrde,
æþeling on elne;   ne wæs ecg bona,
ac him hildegrap   heortan wylmas,
banhus gebræc.   Nu sceall billes ecg,
hond ond heard sweord,   ymb hord wigan."
2510
Beowulf maðelode,   beotwordum spræc
niehstan siðe: "Ic geneðde fela
guða on geogoðe;   gyt ic wylle,
frod folces weard,   fæhðe secan,
mærðu fremman,   gif mec se mansceaða
2515
of eorðsele   ut geseceð."
Gegrette ða   gumena gehwylcne,
hwate helmberend,   hindeman siðe,
swæse gesiðas: "Nolde ic sweord beran,
wæpen to wyrme,   gif ic wiste hu
2520
wið ðam aglæcean   elles meahte
gylpe wiðgripan,   swa ic gio wið Grendle dyde.
Ac ic ðær heaðufyres   hates wene,
oreðes ond attres;   forðon ic me on hafu
bord ond byrnan.   Nelle ic beorges weard
2525
forfleon fotes trem,   ac unc furður sceal
weorðan æt wealle,   swa unc wyrd geteoð,
metod manna gehwæs.   Ic eom on mode from
þæt ic wið þone guðflogan   gylp ofersitte.

184

homestead and house. He had no need
from Swedish realm, or from Spear-Dane folk,
2495
or from men of the Gifths, to get him help, --
some warrior worse for wage to buy!
Ever I fought in the front of all,
sole to the fore; and so shall I fight
while I bide in life and this blade shall last
2500
that early and late hath loyal proved
since for my doughtiness Daeghrefn fell,
slain by my hand, the Hugas' champion.
Nor fared he thence to the Frisian king
with the booty back, and breast-adornments;
2505
but, slain in struggle, that standard-bearer
fell, atheling brave. Not with blade was he slain,
but his bones were broken by brawny gripe,
his heart-waves stilled. -- The sword-edge now,
hard blade and my hand, for the hoard shall strive."
2510
Beowulf spake, and a battle-vow made
his last of all: "I have lived through many
wars in my youth; now once again,
old folk-defender, feud will I seek,
do doughty deeds, if the dark destroyer
2515
forth from his cavern come to fight me!"
Then hailed he the helmeted heroes all,
for the last time greeting his liegemen dear,
comrades of war: "I should carry no weapon,
no sword to the serpent, if sure I knew
2520
how, with such enemy, else my vows
I could gain as I did in Grendel's day.
But fire in this fight I must fear me now,
and poisonous breath; so I bring with me
breastplate and board. {97} From the barrow's keeper
2525
no footbreadth flee I. One fight shall end
our war by the wall, as Wyrd allots,
all mankind's master. My mood is bold
but forbears to boast o'er this battling-flyer.

Gebide ge on beorge   byrnum werede,
2530
secgas on searwum,   hwæðer sel mæge
æfter wælræse   wunde gedygan
uncer twega.   Nis þæt eower sið
ne gemet mannes,   nefne min anes,
þæt he wið aglæcean   eofoðo dæle,
2535
eorlscype efne.   Ic mid elne sceall
gold gegangan,   oððe guð nimeð,
feorhbealu frecne,   frean eowerne!"
Aras ða bi ronde   rof oretta,
heard under helme,   hiorosercean bær
2540
under stancleofu,   strengo getruwode
anes mannes.   Ne bið swylc earges sið!
Geseah ða be wealle   se ðe worna fela,
gumcystum god,   guða gedigde,
hildehlemma,   þonne hnitan feðan,
2545
stondan stanbogan,   stream ut þonan
brecan of beorge.   Wæs þære burnan wælm
heaðofyrum hat;   ne meahte horde neah
unbyrnende   ænige hwile
deop gedygan   for dracan lege.
2550
Let ða of breostum,   ða he gebolgen wæs,
Wedergeata leod   word ut faran,
stearcheort styrmde;   stefn in becom
heaðotorht hlynnan   under harne stan.
Hete wæs onhrered,   hordweard oncniow
2555
mannes reorde;   næs ðær mara fyrst
freode to friclan.   From ærest cwom
oruð aglæcean   ut of stane,
hat hildeswat.   Hruse dynede.
Biorn under beorge   bordrand onswaf
2560
wið ðam gryregieste,   Geata dryhten;
ða wæs hringbogan   heorte gefysed
sæcce to seceanne.   Sweord ær gebræd
god guðcyning,   gomele lafe,
ecgum unslaw;   æghwæðrum wæs

-- Now abide by the barrow, ye breastplate-mailed,
2530
ye heroes in harness, which of us twain
better from battle-rush bear his wounds.
Wait ye the finish. The fight is not yours,
nor meet for any but me alone
to measure might with this monster here
2535
and play the hero. Hardily I
shall win that wealth, or war shall seize,
cruel killing, your king and lord!"
Up stood then with shield the sturdy champion,
stayed by the strength of his single manhood,
2540
and hardy 'neath helmet his harness bore
under cleft of the cliffs: no coward's path!
Soon spied by the wall that warrior chief,
survivor of many a victory-field
where foemen fought with furious clashings,
2545
an arch of stone; and within, a stream
that broke from the barrow. The brooklet's wave
was hot with fire. The hoard that way
he never could hope unharmed to near,
or endure those deeps, {98} for the dragon's flame.
2550
Then let from his breast, for he burst with rage,
the Weder-Geat prince a word outgo;
stormed the stark-heart; stern went ringing
and clear his cry 'neath the cliff-rocks gray.
The hoard-guard heard a human voice;
2555
his rage was enkindled. No respite now
for pact of peace! The poison-breath
of that foul worm first came forth from the cave,
hot reek-of-fight: the rocks resounded.
Stout by the stone-way his shield he raised,
2560
lord of the Geats, against the loathed-one;
while with courage keen that coiled foe
came seeking strife. The sturdy king
had drawn his sword, not dull of edge,
heirloom old; and each of the two

2565
bealohycgendra   broga fram oðrum.
Stiðmod gestod   wið steapne rond
winia bealdor,   ða se wyrm gebeah
snude tosomne;   he on searwum bad.
Gewat ða byrnende   gebogen scriðan,
2570
to gescipe scyndan.   Scyld wel gebearg
life ond lice   læssan hwile
mærum þeodne   þonne his myne sohte,
ðær he þy fyrste,   forman dogore
wealdan moste   swa him wyrd ne gescraf
2575
hreð æt hilde.   Hond up abræd
Geata dryhten,   gryrefahne sloh
incgelafe,   þæt sio ecg gewac
brun on bane,   bat unswiðor
þonne his ðiodcyning   þearfe hæfde,
2580
bysigum gebæded.   þa wæs beorges weard
æfter heaðuswenge   on hreoum mode,
wearp wælfyre;   wide sprungon
hildeleoman.   Hreðsigora ne gealp
goldwine Geata;   guðbill geswac,
2585
nacod æt niðe,   swa hyt no sceolde,
iren ærgod.   Ne wæs þæt eðe sið,
þæt se mæra   maga Ecgðeowes
grundwong þone   ofgyfan wolde;
sceolde ofer willan   wic eardian
2590
elles hwergen,   swa sceal æghwylc mon
alætan lændagas.   Næs ða long to ðon
þæt ða aglæcean hy   eft gemetton.
Hyrte hyne hordweard   (hreðer æðme weoll)
niwan stefne;   nearo ðrowode,
2595
fyre befongen,   se ðe ær folce weold.
Nealles him on heape   handgesteallan,
æðelinga bearn,   ymbe gestodon
hildecystum,   ac hy on holt bugon,
ealdre burgan.   Hiora in anum weoll

2565
felt fear of his foe, though fierce their mood.
Stoutly stood with his shield high-raised
the warrior king, as the worm now coiled
together amain: the mailed-one waited.
Now, spire by spire, fast sped and glided
2570
that blazing serpent. The shield protected,
soul and body a shorter while
for the hero-king than his heart desired,
could his will have wielded the welcome respite
but once in his life! But Wyrd denied it,
2575
and victory's honors. -- His arm he lifted
lord of the Geats, the grim foe smote
with atheling's heirloom. Its edge was turned
brown blade, on the bone, and bit more feebly
than its noble master had need of then
2580
in his baleful stress. -- Then the barrow's keeper
waxed full wild for that weighty blow,
cast deadly flames; wide drove and far
those vicious fires. No victor's glory
the Geats' lord boasted; his brand had failed,
2585
naked in battle, as never it should,
excellent iron! -- 'Twas no easy path
that Ecgtheow's honored heir must tread
over the plain to the place of the foe;
for against his will he must win a home
2590
elsewhere far, as must all men, leaving
this lapsing life! -- Not long it was
ere those champions grimly closed again.
The hoard-guard was heartened; high heaved his breast
once more; and by peril was pressed again,
2595
enfolded in flames, the folk-commander!
Nor yet about him his band of comrades,
sons of athelings, armed stood
with warlike front: to the woods they bent them,
their lives to save. But the soul of one

2600
sefa wið sorgum;   sibb æfre ne mæg
wiht onwendan   þam ðe wel þenceð.

2600
with care was cumbered. Kinship true
can never be marred in a noble mind!

Wiglaf wæs haten   Weoxstanes sunu,
leoflic lindwiga,   leod Scylfinga,
mæg ælfheres;   geseah his mondryhten
2605
under heregriman   hat þrowian.
Gemunde ða ða are   þe he him ær forgeaf,
wicstede weligne   Wægmundinga,
folcrihta gehwylc,   swa his fæder ahte.
Ne mihte ða forhabban;   hond rond gefeng,
2610
geolwe linde,   gomel swyrd geteah,
þæt wæs mid eldum   Eanmundes laf,
suna Ohteres.   þam æt sæcce wearð,
wræccan wineleasum,   Weohstan bana
meces ecgum,   ond his magum ætbær
2615
brunfagne helm,   hringde byrnan,
eald sweord etonisc;   þæt him Onela forgeaf,
his gædelinges   guðgewædu,
fyrdsearo fuslic,   no ymbe ða fæhðe spræc,
þeah ðe he his broðor bearn   abredwade.
2620
He frætwe geheold   fela missera,
bill ond byrnan,   oððæt his byre mihte
eorlscipe efnan   swa his ærfæder;
geaf him ða mid Geatum   guðgewæda,
æghwæs unrim,   þa he of ealdre gewat,
2625
frod on forðweg.   þa wæs forma sið
geongan cempan,   þæt he guðe ræs
mid his freodryhtne   fremman sceolde.
Ne gemealt him se modsefa,   ne his mæges laf
gewac æt wige;   þæt se wyrm onfand,
2630
syððan hie togædre   gegan hæfdon.
Wiglaf maðelode,   wordrihta fela
sægde gesiðum   (him wæs sefa geomor):
"Ic ðæt mæl geman,   þær we medu þegun,
þonne we geheton   ussum hlaforde

XXXVI. WIGLAF HELPS BEOWULF IN THE FEUD.

WIGLAF his name was, Weohstan's son,
linden-thane loved, the lord of Scylfings,
Aelfhere's kinsman. His king he now saw
2605
with heat under helmet hard oppressed.
He minded the prizes his prince had given him,
wealthy seat of the Waegmunding line,
and folk-rights that his father owned
Not long he lingered. The linden yellow,
2610
his shield, he seized; the old sword he drew: --
as heirloom of Eanmund earth-dwellers knew it,
who was slain by the sword-edge, son of Ohtere,
friendless exile, erst in fray
killed by Weohstan, who won for his kin
2615
brown-bright helmet, breastplate ringed,
old sword of Eotens, Onela's gift,
weeds of war of the warrior-thane,
battle-gear brave: though a brother's child
had been felled, the feud was unfelt by Onela. {99}
2620
For winters this war-gear Weohstan kept,
breastplate and board, till his bairn had grown
earlship to earn as the old sire did:
then he gave him, mid Geats, the gear of battle,
portion huge, when he passed from life,
2625
fared aged forth. For the first time now
with his leader-lord the liegeman young
was bidden to share the shock of battle.
Neither softened his soul, nor the sire's bequest
weakened in war. {100} So the worm found out
2630
when once in fight the foes had met!
Wiglaf spake, -- and his words were sage;
sad in spirit, he said to his comrades: --
"I remember the time, when mead we took,
what promise we made to this prince of ours

2635
in biorsele,   ðe us ðas beagas geaf,
þæt we him ða guðgetawa   gyldan woldon
gif him þyslicu   þearf gelumpe,
helmas ond heard sweord.   ðe he usic on herge geceas
to ðyssum siðfate   sylfes willum,
2640
onmunde usic mærða,   ond me þas maðmas geaf,
þe he usic garwigend   gode tealde,
hwate helmberend,   þeah ðe hlaford us
þis ellenweorc   ana aðohte
to gefremmanne,   folces hyrde,
2645
for ðam he manna mæst   mærða gefremede,
dæda dollicra.   Nu is se dæg cumen
þæt ure mandryhten   mægenes behofað,
godra guðrinca;   wutun gongan to,
helpan hildfruman,   þenden hyt sy,
2650
gledegesa grim.   God wat on mec
þæt me is micle leofre   þæt minne lichaman
mid minne goldgyfan   gled fæðmie.
Ne þynceð me gerysne   þæt we rondas beren
eft to earde,   nemne we æror mægen
2655
fane gefyllan,   feorh ealgian
Wedra ðeodnes.   Ic wat geare
þæt næron ealdgewyrht,   þæt he ana scyle
Geata duguðe   gnorn þrowian,
gesigan æt sæcce;   urum sceal sweord ond helm,
2660
byrne ond beaduscrud,   bam gemæne."
Wod þa þurh þone wælrec,   wigheafolan bær
frean on fultum,   fea worda cwæð:
"Leofa Biowulf,   læst eall tela,
swa ðu on geoguðfeore   geara gecwæde
2665
þæt ðu ne alæte   be ðe lifigendum
dom gedreosan.   Scealt nu dædum rof,
æðeling anhydig,   ealle mægene
feorh ealgian;   ic ðe fullæstu."
æfter ðam wordum   wyrm yrre cwom,

2635
in the banquet-hall, to our breaker-of-rings,
for gear of combat to give him requital,
for hard-sword and helmet, if hap should bring
stress of this sort! Himself who chose us
from all his army to aid him now,
2640
urged us to glory, and gave these treasures,
because he counted us keen with the spear
and hardy 'neath helm, though this hero-work
our leader hoped unhelped and alone
to finish for us, -- folk-defender
2645
who hath got him glory greater than all men
for daring deeds! Now the day is come
that our noble master has need of the might
of warriors stout. Let us stride along
the hero to help while the heat is about him
2650
glowing and grim! For God is my witness
I am far more fain the fire should seize
along with my lord these limbs of mine! {101}
Unsuiting it seems our shields to bear
homeward hence, save here we essay
2655
to fell the foe and defend the life
of the Weders' lord. I wot 'twere shame
on the law of our land if alone the king
out of Geatish warriors woe endured
and sank in the struggle! My sword and helmet,
2660
breastplate and board, for us both shall serve!"
Through slaughter-reek strode he to succor his chieftain,
his battle-helm bore, and brief words spake: --
"Beowulf dearest, do all bravely,
as in youthful days of yore thou vowedst
2665
that while life should last thou wouldst let no wise
thy glory droop! Now, great in deeds,
atheling steadfast, with all thy strength
shield thy life! I will stand to help thee."
At the words the worm came once again,

2670
atol inwitgæst,   oðre siðe
fyrwylmum fah   fionda niosian,
laðra manna;   ligyðum for.
Born bord wið rond,   byrne ne meahte
geongum garwigan   geoce gefremman,
2675
ac se maga geonga   under his mæges scyld
elne geeode,   þa his agen wæs
gledum forgrunden.   þa gen guðcyning
mærða gemunde,   mægenstrengo sloh
hildebille,   þæt hyt on heafolan stod
2680
niþe genyded;   Nægling forbærst,
geswac æt sæcce   sweord Biowulfes,
gomol ond grægmæl.   Him þæt gifeðe ne wæs
þæt him irenna   ecge mihton
helpan æt hilde;   wæs sio hond to strong,
2685
se ðe meca gehwane,   mine gefræge,
swenge ofersohte,   þonne he to sæcce bær
wæpen wundrum heard;   næs him wihte ðe sel.
þa wæs þeodsceaða   þriddan siðe,
frecne fyrdraca,   fæhða gemyndig,
2690
ræsde on ðone rofan,   þa him rum ageald,
hat ond heaðogrim,   heals ealne ymbefeng
biteran banum;   he geblodegod wearð
sawuldriore,   swat yðum weoll.

2670
murderous monster mad with rage,
with fire-billows flaming, its foes to seek,
the hated men. In heat-waves burned
that board {102} to the boss, and the breastplate failed
to shelter at all the spear-thane young.
2675
Yet quickly under his kinsman's shield
went eager the earl, since his own was now
all burned by the blaze. The bold king again
had mind of his glory: with might his glaive
was driven into the dragon's head, --
2680
blow nerved by hate. But Naegling {103} was shivered,
broken in battle was Beowulf's sword,
old and gray. 'Twas granted him not
that ever the edge of iron at all
could help him at strife: too strong was his hand,
2685
so the tale is told, and he tried too far
with strength of stroke all swords he wielded,
though sturdy their steel: they steaded him nought.
Then for the third time thought on its feud
that folk-destroyer, fire-dread dragon,
2690
and rushed on the hero, where room allowed,
battle-grim, burning; its bitter teeth
closed on his neck, and covered him
with waves of blood from his breast that welled.

Ða ic æt þearfe gefrægn   þeodcyninges
2695
andlongne eorl   ellen cyðan,
cræft ond cenðu,   swa him gecynde wæs.
Ne hedde he þæs heafolan,   ac sio hand gebarn
modiges mannes,   þær he his mæges healp,
þæt he þone niðgæst   nioðor hwene sloh,
2700
secg on searwum,   þæt ðæt sweord gedeaf,
fah ond fæted,   þæt ðæt fyr ongon
sweðrian syððan.   þa gen sylf cyning
geweold his gewitte,   wællseaxe gebræd
biter ond beaduscearp,   þæt he on byrnan wæg;
2705
forwrat Wedra helm   wyrm on middan.
Feond gefyldan   (ferh ellen wræc),
ond hi hyne þa begen   abroten hæfdon,
sibæðelingas.   Swylc sceolde secg wesan,
þegn æt ðearfe!   þæt ðam þeodne wæs
2710
siðast sigehwila   sylfes dædum,
worlde geweorces.   ða sio wund ongon,
þe him se eorðdraca   ær geworhte,
swelan ond swellan;   he þæt sona onfand,
þæt him on breostum   bealoniðe weoll
2715
attor on innan.   ða se æðeling giong
þæt he bi wealle   wishycgende
gesæt on sesse;   seah on enta geweorc,
hu ða stanbogan   stapulum fæste
ece eorðreced   innan healde.
2720
Hyne þa mid handa   heorodreorigne,
þeoden mærne,   þegn ungemete till
winedryhten his   wætere gelafede,
hilde sædne,   ond his helm onspeon.
Biowulf maþelode   (he ofer benne spræc,
2725
wunde wælbleate;   wisse he gearwe
þæt he dæghwila   gedrogen hæfde,

XXXVII. BEOWULF WOUNDED TO DEATH.

'TWAS now, men say, in his sovran's need
2695
that the earl made known his noble strain,
craft and keenness and courage enduring.
Heedless of harm, though his hand was burned,
hardy-hearted, he helped his kinsman.
A little lower the loathsome beast
2700
he smote with sword; his steel drove in
bright and burnished; that blaze began
to lose and lessen. At last the king
wielded his wits again, war-knife drew,
a biting blade by his breastplate hanging,
2705
and the Weders'-helm smote that worm asunder,
felled the foe, flung forth its life.
So had they killed it, kinsmen both,
athelings twain: thus an earl should be
in danger's day! -- Of deeds of valor
2710
this conqueror's-hour of the king was last,
of his work in the world. The wound began,
which that dragon-of-earth had erst inflicted,
to swell and smart; and soon he found
in his breast was boiling, baleful and deep,
2715
pain of poison. The prince walked on,
wise in his thought, to the wall of rock;
then sat, and stared at the structure of giants,
where arch of stone and steadfast column
upheld forever that hall in earth.
2720
Yet here must the hand of the henchman peerless
lave with water his winsome lord,
the king and conqueror covered with blood,
with struggle spent, and unspan his helmet.
Beowulf spake in spite of his hurt,
2725
his mortal wound; full well he knew
his portion now was past and gone

eorðan wynne;   ða wæs eall sceacen
dogorgerimes,   deað ungemete neah):
"Nu ic suna minum   syllan wolde
2730
guðgewædu,   þær me gifeðe swa
ænig yrfeweard   æfter wurde
lice gelenge.   Ic ðas leode heold
fiftig wintra;   næs se folccyning,
ymbesittendra   ænig ðara,
2735
þe mec guðwinum   gretan dorste,
egesan ðeon.   Ic on earde bad
mælgesceafta,   heold min tela,
ne sohte searoniðas,   ne me swor fela
aða on unriht.   Ic ðæs ealles mæg
2740
feorhbennum seoc   gefean habban;
for ðam me witan ne ðearf   waldend fira
morðorbealo maga,   þonne min sceaceð
lif of lice.   Nu ðu lungre geong
hord sceawian   under harne stan,
2745
Wiglaf leofa,   nu se wyrm ligeð,
swefeð sare wund,   since bereafod.
Bio nu on ofoste,   þæt ic ærwelan,
goldæht ongite,   gearo sceawige
swegle searogimmas,   þæt ic ðy seft mæge
2750
æfter maððumwelan   min alætan
lif ond leodscipe,   þone ic longe heold."

of earthly bliss, and all had fled
of his file of days, and death was near:
"I would fain bestow on son of mine
2730
this gear of war, were given me now
that any heir should after me come
of my proper blood. This people I ruled
fifty winters. No folk-king was there,
none at all, of the neighboring clans
2735
who war would wage me with 'warriors'-friends' {104}
and threat me with horrors. At home I bided
what fate might come, and I cared for mine own;
feuds I sought not, nor falsely swore
ever on oath. For all these things,
2740
though fatally wounded, fain am I!
From the Ruler-of-Man no wrath shall seize me,
when life from my frame must flee away,
for killing of kinsmen! Now quickly go
and gaze on that hoard 'neath the hoary rock,
2745
Wiglaf loved, now the worm lies low,
sleeps, heart-sore, of his spoil bereaved.
And fare in haste. I would fain behold
the gorgeous heirlooms, golden store,
have joy in the jewels and gems, lay down
2750
softlier for sight of this splendid hoard
my life and the lordship I long have held."

Ða ic snude gefrægn   sunu Wihstanes
æfter wordcwydum   wundum dryhtne
hyran heaðosiocum,   hringnet beran,
2755
brogdne beadusercean   under beorges hrof.
Geseah ða sigehreðig,   þa he bi sesse geong,
magoþegn modig   maððumsigla fealo,
gold glitinian   grunde getenge,
wundur on wealle,   ond þæs wyrmes denn,
2760
ealdes uhtflogan,   orcas stondan,
fyrnmanna fatu   feormendlease,
hyrstum behrorene;   þær wæs helm monig
eald ond omig,   earmbeaga fela
searwum gesæled.   Sinc eaðe mæg,
2765
gold on grunde,   gumcynnes gehwone
oferhigian,   hyde se ðe wylle.
Swylce he siomian geseah   segn eallgylden
heah ofer horde,   hondwundra mæst,
gelocen leoðocræftum;   of ðam leoma stod,
2770
þæt he þone grundwong   ongitan meahte,
wræte giondwlitan.   Næs ðæs wyrmes þær
onsyn ænig,   ac hyne ecg fornam.
ða ic on hlæwe gefrægn   hord reafian,
eald enta geweorc,   anne mannan,
2775
him on bearm hladon   bunan ond discas
sylfes dome;   segn eac genom,
beacna beorhtost.   Bill ær gescod
(ecg wæs iren)   ealdhlafordes
þam ðara maðma   mundbora wæs
2780
longe hwile,   ligegesan wæg
hatne for horde,   hioroweallende
middelnihtum,   oðþæt he morðre swealt.
Ar wæs on ofoste,   eftsiðes georn,
frætwum gefyrðred;   hyne fyrwet bræc,
2785

XXXVIII. THE JEWEL-HOARD.
-THE PASSING OF BEOWULF.

I HAVE heard that swiftly the son of Weohstan
at wish and word of his wounded king, --
war-sick warrior, -- woven mail-coat,
2755
battle-sark, bore 'neath the barrow's roof.
Then the clansman keen, of conquest proud,
passing the seat, {105} saw store of jewels
and glistening gold the ground along;
by the wall were marvels, and many a vessel
2760
in the den of the dragon, the dawn-flier old:
unburnished bowls of bygone men
reft of richness; rusty helms
of the olden age; and arm-rings many
wondrously woven. -- Such wealth of gold,
2765
booty from barrow, can burden with pride
each human wight: let him hide it who will! --
His glance too fell on a gold-wove banner
high o'er the hoard, of handiwork noblest,
brilliantly broidered; so bright its gleam,
2770
all the earth-floor he easily saw
and viewed all these vessels. No vestige now
was seen of the serpent: the sword had ta'en him.
Then, I heard, the hill of its hoard was reft,
old work of giants, by one alone;
2775
he burdened his bosom with beakers and plate
at his own good will, and the ensign took,
brightest of beacons. -- The blade of his lord
-- its edge was iron -- had injured deep
one that guarded the golden hoard
2780
many a year and its murder-fire
spread hot round the barrow in horror-billows
at midnight hour, till it met its doom.
Hasted the herald, the hoard so spurred him
his track to retrace; he was troubled by doubt,
2785

hwæðer collenferð   cwicne gemette
in ðam wongstede   Wedra þeoden
ellensiocne,   þær he hine ær forlet.
He ða mid þam maðmum   mærne þioden,
dryhten sinne,   driorigne fand
2790
ealdres æt ende;   he hine eft ongon
wæteres weorpan,   oðþæt wordes ord
breosthord þurhbræc.
gomel on giohðe   (gold sceawode):
"Ic ðara frætwa   frean ealles ðanc,
2795
wuldurcyninge,   wordum secge,
ecum dryhtne,   þe ic her on starie,
þæs ðe ic moste   minum leodum
ær swyltdæge   swylc gestrynan.
Nu ic on maðma hord   mine bebohte
2800
frode feorhlege,   fremmað gena
leoda þearfe;   ne mæg ic her leng wesan.
Hatað heaðomære   hlæw gewyrcean
beorhtne æfter bæle   æt brimes nosan;
se scel to gemyndum   minum leodum
2805
heah hlifian   on Hronesnæsse,
þæt hit sæliðend   syððan hatan
Biowulfes biorh,   ða ðe brentingas
ofer floda genipu   feorran drifað."
Dyde him of healse   hring gyldenne
2810
þioden þristhydig,   þegne gesealde,
geongum garwigan,   goldfahne helm,
beah ond byrnan,   het hyne brucan well:
"þu eart endelaf   usses cynnes,
Wægmundinga.   Ealle wyrd forsweop
2815
mine magas   to metodsceafte,
eorlas on elne;   ic him æfter sceal."
þæt wæs þam gomelan   gingæste word
breostgehygdum,   ær he bæl cure,
hate heaðowylmas;   him of hreðre gewat
2820
sawol secean   soðfæstra dom.

high-souled hero, if haply he'd find
alive, where he left him, the lord of Weders,
weakening fast by the wall of the cave.
So he carried the load. His lord and king
he found all bleeding, famous chief
2790
at the lapse of life. The liegeman again
plashed him with water, till point of word
broke through the breast-hoard. Beowulf spake,
sage and sad, as he stared at the gold. --
"For the gold and treasure, to God my thanks,
2795
to the Wielder-of-Wonders, with words I say,
for what I behold, to Heaven's Lord,
for the grace that I give such gifts to my folk
or ever the day of my death be run!
Now I've bartered here for booty of treasure
2800
the last of my life, so look ye well
to the needs of my land! No longer I tarry.
A barrow bid ye the battle-fanned raise
for my ashes. 'Twill shine by the shore of the flood,
to folk of mine memorial fair
2805
on Hrones Headland high uplifted,
that ocean-wanderers oft may hail
Beowulf's Barrow, as back from far
they drive their keels o'er the darkling wave."
From his neck he unclasped the collar of gold,
2810
valorous king, to his vassal gave it
with bright-gold helmet, breastplate, and ring,
to the youthful thane: bade him use them in joy.
"Thou art end and remnant of all our race
the Waegmunding name. For Wyrd hath swept them,
2815
all my line, to the land of doom,
earls in their glory: I after them go."
This word was the last which the wise old man
harbored in heart ere hot death-waves
of balefire he chose. From his bosom fled
2820
his soul to seek the saints' reward.

Ða wæs gegongen   guman unfrodum
earfoðlice,   þæt he on eorðan geseah
þone leofestan   lifes æt ende
bleate gebæran.   Bona swylce læg,
2825
egeslic eorðdraca   ealdre bereafod,
bealwe gebæded.   Beahhordum leng
wyrm wohbogen   wealdan ne moste,
ac hine irenna   ecga fornamon,
hearde, heaðoscearde   homera lafe,
2830
þæt se widfloga   wundum stille
hreas on hrusan   hordærne neah.
Nalles æfter lyfte   lacende hwearf
middelnihtum,   maðmæhta wlonc
ansyn ywde,   ac he eorðan gefeoll
2835
for ðæs hildfruman   hondgeweorce.
Huru þæt on lande   lyt manna ðah,
mægenagendra,   mine gefræge,
þeah ðe he dæda gehwæs   dyrstig wære,
þæt he wið attorsceaðan   oreðe geræsde,
2840
oððe hringsele   hondum styrede,
gif he wæccende   weard onfunde
buon on beorge.   Biowulfe wearð
dryhtmaðma dæl   deaðe forgolden;
hæfde æghwæðer   ende gefered
2845
lænan lifes.   Næs ða lang to ðon
þæt ða hildlatan   holt ofgefan,
tydre treowlogan   tyne ætsomne.
ða ne dorston ær   dareðum lacan
on hyra mandryhtnes   miclan þearfe,
2850
ac hy scamiende   scyldas bæran,
guðgewædu,   þær se gomela læg,
wlitan on Wilaf.   He gewergad sæt,
feðecempa,   frean eaxlum neah,
wehte hyne wætre;   him wiht ne speow.

XXXIX. THE COWARD THANES.

IT was heavy hap for that hero young
on his lord beloved to look and find him
lying on earth with life at end,
sorrowful sight. But the slayer too,
2825
awful earth-dragon, empty of breath,
lay felled in fight, nor, fain of its treasure,
could the writhing monster rule it more.
For edges of iron had ended its days,
hard and battle-sharp, hammers' leaving; {106}
2830
and that flier-afar had fallen to ground
hushed by its hurt, its hoard all near,
no longer lusty aloft to whirl
at midnight, making its merriment seen,
proud of its prizes: prone it sank
2835
by the handiwork of the hero-king.
Forsooth among folk but few achieve,
-- though sturdy and strong, as stories tell me,
and never so daring in deed of valor, --
the perilous breath of a poison-foe
2840
to brave, and to rush on the ring-board hall,
whenever his watch the warden keeps
bold in the barrow. Beowulf paid
the price of death for that precious hoard;
and each of the foes had found the end
2845
of this fleeting life. Befell erelong
that the laggards in war the wood had left,
trothbreakers, cowards, ten together,
fearing before to flourish a spear
in the sore distress of their sovran lord.
2850
Now in their shame their shields they carried,
armor of fight, where the old man lay;
and they gazed on Wiglaf. Wearied he sat
at his sovran's shoulder, shieldsman good,
to wake him with water. {107} Nowise it availed.

2855
Ne meahte he on eorðan,   ðeah he uðe wel,
on ðam frumgare   feorh gehealdan,
ne ðæs wealdendes   wiht oncirran;
wolde dom godes   dædum rædan
gumena gehwylcum,   swa he nu gen deð.
2860
þa wæs æt ðam geongan   grim ondswaru
eðbegete   þam ðe ær his elne forleas.
Wiglaf maðelode,   Weohstanes sunu,
sec, sarigferð   (seah on unleofe):
"þæt, la, mæg secgan   se ðe wyle soð specan
2865
þæt se mondryhten   se eow ða maðmas geaf,
eoredgeatwe,   þe ge þær on standað,
þonne he on ealubence   oft gesealde
healsittendum   helm ond byrnan,
þeoden his þegnum,   swylce he þrydlicost
2870
ower feor oððe neah   findan meahte,
þæt he genunga   guðgewædu
wraðe forwurpe,   ða hyne wig beget.
Nealles folccyning   fyrdgesteallum
gylpan þorfte;   hwæðre him god uðe,
2875
sigora waldend,   þæt he hyne sylfne gewræc
ana mid ecge,   þa him wæs elnes þearf.
Ic him lifwraðe   lytle meahte
ætgifan æt guðe,   ond ongan swa þeah
ofer min gemet   mæges helpan;
2880
symle wæs þy sæmra,   þonne ic sweorde drep
ferhðgeniðlan,   fyr unswiðor
weoll of gewitte.   Wergendra to lyt
þrong ymbe þeoden,   þa hyne sio þrag becwom.
Nu sceal sincþego   ond swyrdgifu,
2885
eall eðelwyn   eowrum cynne,
lufen alicgean;   londrihtes mot
þære mægburge   monna æghwylc
idel hweorfan,   syððan æðelingas
feorran gefricgean   fleam eowerne,

2855
Though well he wished it, in world no more
could he barrier life for that leader-of-battles
nor baffle the will of all-wielding God.
Doom of the Lord was law o'er the deeds
of every man, as it is to-day.
2860
Grim was the answer, easy to get,
from the youth for those that had yielded to fear!
Wiglaf spake, the son of Weohstan, --
mournful he looked on those men unloved: --
"Who sooth will speak, can say indeed
2865
that the ruler who gave you golden rings
and the harness of war in which ye stand
-- for he at ale-bench often-times
bestowed on hall-folk helm and breastplate,
lord to liegemen, the likeliest gear
2870
which near of far he could find to give, --
threw away and wasted these weeds of battle,
on men who failed when the foemen came!
Not at all could the king of his comrades-in-arms
venture to vaunt, though the Victory-Wielder,
2875
God, gave him grace that he got revenge
sole with his sword in stress and need.
To rescue his life, 'twas little that I
could serve him in struggle; yet shift I made
(hopeless it seemed) to help my kinsman.
2880
Its strength ever waned, when with weapon I struck
that fatal foe, and the fire less strongly
flowed from its head. -- Too few the heroes
in throe of contest that thronged to our king!
Now gift of treasure and girding of sword,
2885
joy of the house and home-delight
shall fail your folk; his freehold-land
every clansman within your kin
shall lose and leave, when lords high-born
hear afar of that flight of yours,

2890
domleasan dæd.   Deað bið sella
eorla gehwylcum   þonne edwitlif!"

2890
a fameless deed. Yea, death is better
for liegemen all than a life of shame!"

Heht ða þæt heaðoweorc   to hagan biodan
up ofer ecgclif,   þær þæt eorlweorod
morgenlongne dæg   modgiomor sæt,
2895
bordhæbbende,   bega on wenum,
endedogores   ond eftcymes
leofes monnes.   Lyt swigode
niwra spella   se ðe næs gerad,
ac he soðlice   sægde ofer ealle:
2900
"Nu is wilgeofa   Wedra leoda,
dryhten Geata,   deaðbedde fæst,
wunað wælreste   wyrmes dædum.
Him on efn ligeð   ealdorgewinna
sexbennum seoc;   sweorde ne meahte
2905
on ðam aglæcean   ænige þinga
wunde gewyrcean.   Wiglaf siteð
ofer Biowulfe,   byre Wihstanes,
eorl ofer oðrum   unlifigendum,
healdeð higemæðum   heafodwearde
2910
leofes ond laðes.   Nu ys leodum wen
orleghwile,   syððan underne
Froncum ond Frysum   fyll cyninges
wide weorðeð.   Wæs sio wroht scepen
heard wið Hugas,   syððan Higelac cwom
2915
faran flotherge   on Fresna land,
þær hyne Hetware   hilde genægdon,
elne geeodon   mid ofermægene,
þæt se byrnwiga   bugan sceolde,
feoll on feðan,   nalles frætwe geaf
2920
ealdor dugoðe.   Us wæs a syððan
Merewioingas   milts ungyfeðe.
Ne ic to Sweoðeode   sibbe oððe treowe
wihte ne wene,   ac wæs wide cuð
þætte Ongenðio   ealdre besnyðede
2925
Hæðcen Hreþling   wið Hrefnawudu,

XL. THE SOLDIER'S DIRGE AND PROPHECY.

THAT battle-toil bade he at burg to announce,
at the fort on the cliff, where, full of sorrow,
all the morning earls had sat,
2895
daring shieldsmen, in doubt of twain:
would they wail as dead, or welcome home,
their lord beloved? Little {108} kept back
of the tidings new, but told them all,
the herald that up the headland rode. --
2900
"Now the willing-giver to Weder folk
in death-bed lies; the Lord of Geats
on the slaughter-bed sleeps by the serpent's deed!
And beside him is stretched that slayer-of-men
with knife-wounds sick: {109} no sword availed
2905
on the awesome thing in any wise
to work a wound. There Wiglaf sitteth,
Weohstan's bairn, by Beowulf's side,
the living earl by the other dead,
and heavy of heart a head-watch {110} keeps
2910
o'er friend and foe. -- Now our folk may look
for waging of war when once unhidden
to Frisian and Frank the fall of the king
is spread afar. -- The strife began
when hot on the Hugas {111} Hygelac fell
2915
and fared with his fleet to the Frisian land.
Him there the Hetwaras humbled in war,
plied with such prowess their power o'erwhelming
that the bold-in-battle bowed beneath it
and fell in fight. To his friends no wise
2920
could that earl give treasure! And ever since
the Merowings' favor has failed us wholly.
Nor aught expect I of peace and faith
from Swedish folk. 'Twas spread afar
how Ongentheow reft at Ravenswood
2925
Haethcyn Hrethling of hope and life,

þa for onmedlan   ærest gesohton
Geata leode   Guðscilfingas.
Sona him se froda   fæder Ohtheres,
eald ond egesfull,   ondslyht ageaf,
2930
abreot brimwisan,   bryd ahredde,
gomela iomeowlan   golde berofene,
Onelan modor   ond Ohtheres,
ond ða folgode   feorhgeniðlan,
oððæt hi oðeodon   earfoðlice
2935
in Hrefnesholt   hlafordlease.
Besæt ða sinherge   sweorda lafe,
wundum werge,   wean oft gehet
earmre teohhe   ondlonge niht,
cwæð, he on mergenne   meces ecgum
2940
getan wolde,   sum on galgtreowum
fuglum to gamene.   Frofor eft gelamp
sarigmodum   somod ærdæge,
syððan hie Hygelaces   horn ond byman,
gealdor ongeaton,   þa se goda com
2945
leoda dugoðe   on last faran.

when the folk of Geats for the first time sought
in wanton pride the Warlike-Scylfings.
Soon the sage old sire {112} of Ohtere,
ancient and awful, gave answering blow;
2930
the sea-king {113} he slew, and his spouse redeemed,
his good wife rescued, though robbed of her gold,
mother of Ohtere and Onela.
Then he followed his foes, who fled before him
sore beset and stole their way,
2935
bereft of a ruler, to Ravenswood.
With his host he besieged there what swords had left,
the weary and wounded; woes he threatened
the whole night through to that hard-pressed throng:
some with the morrow his sword should kill,
2940
some should go to the gallows-tree
for rapture of ravens. But rescue came
with dawn of day for those desperate men
when they heard the horn of Hygelac sound,
tones of his trumpet; the trusty king
2945
had followed their trail with faithful band.

Wæs sio swatswaðu   Sweona ond Geata,
wælræs weora   wide gesyne,
hu ða folc mid him   fæhðe towehton.
Gewat him ða se goda   mid his gædelingum,
2950
frod, felageomor,   fæsten secean,
eorl Ongenþio,   ufor oncirde;
hæfde Higelaces   hilde gefrunen,
wlonces wigcræft,   wiðres ne truwode,
þæt he sæmannum   onsacan mihte,
2955
heaðoliðendum   hord forstandan,
bearn ond bryde;   beah eft þonan
eald under eorðweall.   þa wæs æht boden
Sweona leodum,   segn Higelaces
freoðowong þone   forð ofereodon,
2960
syððan Hreðlingas   to hagan þrungon.
þær wearð Ongenðiow   ecgum sweorda,
blondenfexa,   on bid wrecen,
þæt se þeodcyning   ðafian sceolde
Eafores anne dom.   Hyne yrringa
2965
Wulf Wonreding   wæpne geræhte,
þæt him for swenge   swat ædrum sprong
forð under fexe.   Næs he forht swa ðeh,
gomela Scilfing,   ac forgeald hraðe
wyrsan wrixle   wælhlem þone,
2970
syððan ðeodcyning   þyder oncirde.
Ne meahte se snella   sunu Wonredes
ealdum ceorle   ondslyht giofan,
ac he him on heafde   helm ær gescer,
þæt he blode fah   bugan sceolde,
2975
feoll on foldan;   næs he fæge þa git,
ac he hyne gewyrpte,   þeah ðe him wund hrine.
Let se hearda   Higelaces þegn
bradne mece,   þa his broðor læg,
eald sweord eotonisc,   entiscne helm

XLI. HE TELLS OF THE SWEDES AND THE GEATS.

"THE bloody swath of Swedes and Geats
and the storm of their strife, were seen afar,
how folk against folk the fight had wakened.
The ancient king with his atheling band
2950
sought his citadel, sorrowing much:
Ongentheow earl went up to his burg.
He had tested Hygelac's hardihood,
the proud one's prowess, would prove it no longer,
defied no more those fighting-wanderers
2955
nor hoped from the seamen to save his hoard,
his bairn and his bride: so he bent him again,
old, to his earth-walls. Yet after him came
with slaughter for Swedes the standards of Hygelac
o'er peaceful plains in pride advancing,
2960
till Hrethelings fought in the fenced town. {114}
Then Ongentheow with edge of sword,
the hoary-bearded, was held at bay,
and the folk-king there was forced to suffer
Eofor's anger. In ire, at the king
2965
Wulf Wonreding with weapon struck;
and the chieftain's blood, for that blow, in streams
flowed 'neath his hair. No fear felt he,
stout old Scylfing, but straightway repaid
in better bargain that bitter stroke
2970
and faced his foe with fell intent.
Nor swift enough was the son of Wonred
answer to render the aged chief;
too soon on his head the helm was cloven;
blood-bedecked he bowed to earth,
2975
and fell adown; not doomed was he yet,
and well he waxed, though the wound was sore.
Then the hardy Hygelac-thane, {115}
when his brother fell, with broad brand smote,
giants' sword crashing through giants'-helm

2980
brecan ofer bordweal;   ða gebeah cyning,
folces hyrde,   wæs in feorh dropen.
ða wæron monige   þe his mæg wriðon,
ricone arærdon,   ða him gerymed wearð
þæt hie wælstowe   wealdan moston.
2985
þenden reafode   rinc oðerne,
nam on Ongenðio   irenbyrnan,
heard swyrd hilted   ond his helm somod,
hares hyrste   Higelace bær.
He ðam frætwum feng   ond him fægre gehet
2990
leana mid leodum,   ond gelæste swa;
geald þone guðræs   Geata dryhten,
Hreðles eafora,   þa he to ham becom,
Iofore ond Wulfe   mid ofermaðmum,
sealde hiora gehwæðrum   hund þusenda
2995
landes ond locenra beaga   (ne ðorfte him ða lean
oðwitan
mon on middangearde),   syððan hie ða mærða
geslogon,
ond ða Iofore forgeaf   angan dohtor,
hamweorðunge,   hyldo to wedde.
þæt ys sio fæhðo   ond se feondscipe,
3000
wælnið wera,   ðæs ðe ic wen hafo,
þe us seceað to   Sweona leoda,
syððan hie gefricgeað   frean userne
ealdorleasne,   þone ðe ær geheold
wið hettendum   hord ond rice
3005
æfter hæleða hryre,   hwate Scildingas,
folcred fremede   oððe furður gen
eorlscipe efnde.   Nu is ofost betost
þæt we þeodcyning   þær sceawian
ond þone gebringan,   þe us beagas geaf,
3010
on adfære.   Ne scel anes hwæt
meltan mid þam modigan,   ac þær is maðma hord,
gold unrime   grimme geceapod,
ond nu æt siðestan   sylfes feore

2980
across the shield-wall: sank the king,
his folk's old herdsman, fatally hurt.
There were many to bind the brother's wounds
and lift him, fast as fate allowed
his people to wield the place-of-war.
2985
But Eofor took from Ongentheow,
earl from other, the iron-breastplate,
hard sword hilted, and helmet too,
and the hoar-chief's harness to Hygelac carried,
who took the trappings, and truly promised
2990
rich fee 'mid folk, -- and fulfilled it so.
For that grim strife gave the Geatish lord,

Hrethel's offspring, when home he came,
to Eofor and Wulf a wealth of treasure,
Each of them had a hundred thousand {116}
2995
in land and linked rings; nor at less price reckoned
mid-earth men such mighty deeds!
And to Eofor he gave his only daughter
in pledge of grace, the pride of his home.

"Such is the feud, the foeman's rage,
3000
death-hate of men: so I deem it sure
that the Swedish folk will seek us home
for this fall of their friends, the fighting-Scylfings,
when once they learn that our warrior leader
lifeless lies, who land and hoard
3005
ever defended from all his foes,
furthered his folk's weal, finished his course
a hardy hero. -- Now haste is best,
that we go to gaze on our Geatish lord,
and bear the bountiful breaker-of-rings
3010
to the funeral pyre. No fragments merely
shall burn with the warrior. Wealth of jewels,
gold untold and gained in terror,
treasure at last with his life obtained,

beagas gebohte.   þa sceall brond fretan,
3015
æled þeccean,   nalles eorl wegan
maððum to gemyndum,   ne mægð scyne
habban on healse   hringweorðunge,
ac sceal geomormod,   golde bereafod,
oft nalles æne   elland tredan,
3020
nu se herewisa   hleahtor alegde,
gamen ond gleodream.   Forðon sceall gar wesan
monig, morgenceald,   mundum bewunden,
hæfen on handa,   nalles hearpan sweg
wigend weccean,   ac se wonna hrefn
3025
fus ofer fægum   fela reordian,
earne secgan   hu him æt æte speow,
þenden he wið wulf   wæl reafode."
Swa se secg hwata   secggende wæs
laðra spella;   he ne leag fela
3030
wyrda ne worda.   Weorod eall aras;
eodon unbliðe   under Earnanæs,
wollenteare   wundur sceawian.
Fundon ða on sande   sawulleasne
hlimbed healdan   þone þe him hringas geaf
3035
ærran mælum;   þa wæs endedæg
godum gegongen,   þæt se guðcyning,
Wedra þeoden,   wundordeaðe swealt.
ær hi þær gesegan   syllicran wiht,
wyrm on wonge   wiðerræhtes þær
3040
laðne licgean;   wæs se legdraca
grimlic, gryrefah,   gledum beswæled.
Se wæs fiftiges   fotgemearces
lang on legere,   lyftwynne heold
nihtes hwilum,   nyðer eft gewat
3045
dennes niosian;   wæs ða deaðe fæst,
hæfde eorðscrafa   ende genyttod.
Him big stodan   bunan ond orcas,
discas lagon   ond dyre swyrd,
omige, þurhetone,   swa hie wið eorðan fæðm

all of that booty the brands shall take,
3015
fire shall eat it. No earl must carry
memorial jewel. No maiden fair
shall wreathe her neck with noble ring:
nay, sad in spirit and shorn of her gold,
oft shall she pass o'er paths of exile
3020
now our lord all laughter has laid aside,
all mirth and revel. Many a spear
morning-cold shall be clasped amain,
lifted aloft; nor shall lilt of harp
those warriors wake; but the wan-hued raven,
3025
fain o'er the fallen, his feast shall praise
and boast to the eagle how bravely he ate
when he and the wolf were wasting the slain."
So he told his sorrowful tidings,
and little {117} he lied, the loyal man
3030
of word or of work. The warriors rose;
sad, they climbed to the Cliff-of-Eagles,
went, welling with tears, the wonder to view.
Found on the sand there, stretched at rest,
their lifeless lord, who had lavished rings
3035
of old upon them. Ending-day
had dawned on the doughty-one; death had seized
in woful slaughter the Weders' king.
There saw they, besides, the strangest being,
loathsome, lying their leader near,
3040
prone on the field. The fiery dragon,
fearful fiend, with flame was scorched.
Reckoned by feet, it was fifty measures
in length as it lay. Aloft erewhile
it had revelled by night, and anon come back,
3045
seeking its den; now in death's sure clutch
it had come to the end of its earth-hall joys.
By it there stood the stoups and jars;
dishes lay there, and dear-decked swords
eaten with rust, as, on earth's lap resting,

3050
þusend wintra   þær eardodon.
þonne wæs þæt yrfe,   eacencræftig,
iumonna gold   galdre bewunden,
þæt ðam hringsele   hrinan ne moste
gumena ænig,   nefne god sylfa,
3055
sigora soðcyning,   sealde þam ðe he wolde
(he is manna gehyld)   hord openian,
efne swa hwylcum manna   swa him gemet ðuhte.

3050
a thousand winters they waited there.
For all that heritage huge, that gold
of bygone men, was bound by a spell, {118}
so the treasure-hall could be touched by none
of human kind, -- save that Heaven's King,
3055
God himself, might give whom he would,
Helper of Heroes, the hoard to open, --
even such a man as seemed to him meet.

Þa wæs gesyne   þæt se sið ne ðah
þam ðe unrihte   inne gehydde
3060
wræte under wealle.   Weard ær ofsloh
feara sumne;   þa sio fæhð gewearð
gewrecen wraðlice.   Wundur hwar þonne
eorl ellenrof   ende gefere
lifgesceafta,   þonne leng ne mæg
3065
mon mid his magum   meduseld buan.
Swa wæs Biowulfe,   þa he biorges weard
sohte, searoniðas;   seolfa ne cuðe
þurh hwæt his worulde gedal   weorðan sceolde.
Swa hit oð domes dæg   diope benemdon
3070
þeodnas mære,   þa ðæt þær dydon,
þæt se secg wære   synnum scildig,
hergum geheaðerod,   hellbendum fæst,
wommum gewitnad,   se ðone wong strude,
næs he goldhwæte   gearwor hæfde
3075
agendes est   ær gesceawod.
Wiglaf maðelode,   Wihstanes sunu:
"Oft sceall eorl monig   anes willan
wræc adreogan,   swa us geworden is.
Ne meahton we gelæran   leofne þeoden,
3080
rices hyrde,   ræd ænigne,
þæt he ne grette   goldweard þone,
lete hyne licgean   þær he longe wæs,
wicum wunian   oð woruldende;
heold on heahgesceap.   Hord ys gesceawod,
3085
grimme gegongen;   wæs þæt gifeðe to swið
þe ðone þeodcyning   þyder ontyhte.
Ic wæs þær inne   ond þæt eall geondseh,
recedes geatwa,   þa me gerymed wæs,
nealles swæslice   sið alyfed
3090
inn under eorðweall.   Ic on ofoste gefeng

XLII. WIGLAF SPEAKS.
-THE BUILDING OF THE BALE-FIRE.

A PERILOUS path, it proved, he {119} trod
who heinously hid, that hall within,
3060
wealth under wall! Its watcher had killed
one of a few, {120} and the feud was avenged
in woful fashion. Wondrous seems it,
what manner a man of might and valor
oft ends his life, when the earl no longer
3065
in mead-hall may live with loving friends.
So Beowulf, when that barrow's warden
he sought, and the struggle; himself knew not
in what wise he should wend from the world at last.
For {121} princes potent, who placed the gold,
3070
with a curse to doomsday covered it deep,
so that marked with sin the man should be,
hedged with horrors, in hell-bonds fast,
racked with plagues, who should rob their hoard.
Yet no greed for gold, but the grace of heaven,
3075
ever the king had kept in view. {122}
Wiglaf spake, the son of Weohstan: --
"At the mandate of one, oft warriors many
sorrow must suffer; and so must we.
The people's-shepherd showed not aught
3080
of care for our counsel, king beloved!
That guardian of gold he should grapple not, urged we,
but let him lie where he long had been
in his earth-hall waiting the end of the world,
the hest of heaven. -- This hoard is ours
3085
but grievously gotten; too grim the fate
which thither carried our king and lord.
I was within there, and all I viewed,
the chambered treasure, when chance allowed me
(and my path was made in no pleasant wise)
3090
under the earth-wall. Eager, I seized

micle mid mundum   mægenbyrðenne
hordgestreona,   hider ut ætbær
cyninge minum.   Cwico wæs þa gena,
wis ond gewittig;   worn eall gespræc
3095
gomol on gehðo   ond eowic gretan het,
bæd þæt ge geworhton   æfter wines dædum
in bælstede   beorh þone hean,
micelne ond mærne,   swa he manna wæs
wigend weorðfullost   wide geond eorðan,
3100
þenden he burhwelan   brucan moste.
Uton nu efstan   oðre siðe,
seon ond secean   searogimma geþræc,
wundur under wealle;   ic eow wisige,
þæt ge genoge   neon sceawiað
3105
beagas ond brad gold.   Sie sio bær gearo,
ædre geæfned,   þonne we ut cymen,
ond þonne geferian   frean userne,
leofne mannan,   þær he longe sceal
on ðæs waldendes   wære geþolian."
3110
Het ða gebeodan   byre Wihstanes,
hæle hildedior,   hæleða monegum,
boldagendra,   þæt hie bælwudu
feorran feredon,   folcagende,
godum togenes: "Nu sceal gled fretan,
3115
weaxan wonna leg   wigena strengel,
þone ðe oft gebad   isernscure,
þonne stræla storm   strengum gebæded
scoc ofer scildweall,   sceft nytte heold,
feðergearwum fus   flane fulleode."
3120
Huru se snotra   sunu Wihstanes
acigde of corðre   cyninges þegnas
syfone tosomne,   þa selestan,
eode eahta sum   under inwithrof
hilderinca;   sum on handa bær
3125
æledleoman,   se ðe on orde geong.
Næs ða on hlytme   hwa þæt hord strude,

such heap from the hoard as hands could bear
and hurriedly carried it hither back
to my liege and lord. Alive was he still,
still wielding his wits. The wise old man
3095
spake much in his sorrow, and sent you greetings
and bade that ye build, when he breathed no more,
on the place of his balefire a barrow high,
memorial mighty. Of men was he
worthiest warrior wide earth o'er
3100
the while he had joy of his jewels and burg.
Let us set out in haste now, the second time
to see and search this store of treasure,
these wall-hid wonders, -- the way I show you, --
where, gathered near, ye may gaze your fill
3105
at broad-gold and rings. Let the bier, soon made,
be all in order when out we come,
our king and captain to carry thither
-- man beloved -- where long he shall bide
safe in the shelter of sovran God."
3110
Then the bairn of Weohstan bade command,
hardy chief, to heroes many
that owned their homesteads, hither to bring
firewood from far -- o'er the folk they ruled --
for the famed-one's funeral. " Fire shall devour
3115
and wan flames feed on the fearless warrior
who oft stood stout in the iron-shower,
when, sped from the string, a storm of arrows
shot o'er the shield-wall: the shaft held firm,
featly feathered, followed the barb."
3120
And now the sage young son of Weohstan
seven chose of the chieftain's thanes,
the best he found that band within,
and went with these warriors, one of eight,
under hostile roof. In hand one bore
3125
a lighted torch and led the way.
No lots they cast for keeping the hoard

syððan orwearde   ænigne dæl
secgas gesegon   on sele wunian,
læne licgan;   lyt ænig mearn
3130
þæt hi ofostlice   ut geferedon
dyre maðmas.   Dracan ec scufun,
wyrm ofer weallclif,   leton weg niman,
flod fæðmian   frætwa hyrde.
þa wæs wunden gold   on wæn hladen,
3135
æghwæs unrim,   æþeling boren,
har hilderinc   to Hronesnæsse.

when once the warriors saw it in hall,
altogether without a guardian,
lying there lost. And little they mourned
3130
when they had hastily haled it out,
dear-bought treasure! The dragon they cast,
the worm, o'er the wall for the wave to take,
and surges swallowed that shepherd of gems.
Then the woven gold on a wain was laden --
3135
countless quite! -- and the king was borne,
hoary hero, to Hrones-Ness.

Him ða gegiredan   Geata leode
ad on eorðan   unwaclicne,
helmum behongen,   hildebordum,
3140
beorhtum byrnum,   swa he bena wæs;
alegdon ða tomiddes   mærne þeoden
hæleð hiofende,   hlaford leofne.
Ongunnon þa on beorge   bælfyra mæst
wigend weccan;   wudurec astah,
3145
sweart ofer swioðole,   swogende leg
wope bewunden   (windblond gelæg),
oðþæt he ða banhus   gebrocen hæfde,
hat on hreðre.   Higum unrote
modceare mændon,   mondryhtnes cwealm;
3150
swylce giomorgyd   Geatisc meowle
bundenheorde
song sorgcearig   swiðe geneahhe
þæt hio hyre heofungdagas   hearde ondrede,
wælfylla worn,   werudes egesan,
3155
hynðo ond hæftnyd.   Heofon rece swealg.
Geworhton ða   Wedra leode
hleo on hoe,   se wæs heah ond brad,
wægliðendum   wide gesyne,
ond betimbredon   on tyn dagum
3160
beadurofes becn,   bronda lafe
wealle beworhton,   swa hyt weorðlicost
foresnotre men   findan mihton.
Hi on beorg dydon   beg ond siglu,
eall swylce hyrsta,   swylce on horde ær
3165
niðhedige men   genumen hæfdon,
forleton eorla gestreon   eorðan healdan,
gold on greote,   þær hit nu gen lifað
eldum swa unnyt   swa hit æror wæs.
þa ymbe hlæw riodan   hildediore,
3170
æþelinga bearn,   ealra twelfe,

XLIII. BEOWULF'S FUNERAL PYRE.

THEN fashioned for him the folk of Geats
firm on the earth a funeral-pile,
and hung it with helmets and harness of war
3140
and breastplates bright, as the boon he asked;
and they laid amid it the mighty chieftain,
heroes mourning their master dear.
Then on the hill that hugest of balefires
the warriors wakened. Wood-smoke rose
3145
black over blaze, and blent was the roar
of flame with weeping (the wind was still),
till the fire had broken the frame of bones,
hot at the heart. In heavy mood
their misery moaned they, their master's death.
3150
Wailing her woe, the widow {123} old,
her hair upbound, for Beowulf's death
sung in her sorrow, and said full oft
she dreaded the doleful days to come,
deaths enow, and doom of battle,
3155
and shame. -- The smoke by the sky was devoured.
The folk of the Weders fashioned there
on the headland a barrow broad and high,
by ocean-farers far descried:
in ten days' time their toil had raised it,
3160
the battle-brave's beacon. Round brands of the pyre
a wall they built, the worthiest ever
that wit could prompt in their wisest men.
They placed in the barrow that precious booty,
the rounds and the rings they had reft erewhile,
3165
hardy heroes, from hoard in cave, --
trusting the ground with treasure of earls,
gold in the earth, where ever it lies
useless to men as of yore it was.
Then about that barrow the battle-keen rode,
3170
atheling-born, a band of twelve,

woldon ceare cwiðan   ond kyning mænan,
wordgyd wrecan   ond ymb wer sprecan;
eahtodan eorlscipe   ond his ellenweorc
duguðum demdon,   swa hit gedefe bið
3175
þæt mon his winedryhten   wordum herge,
ferhðum freoge,   þonne he forð scile
of lichaman   læded weorðan.

Swa begnornodon   Geata leode
hlafordes hryre,   heorðgeneatas,
3180
cwædon þæt he wære   wyruldcyninga
manna mildust   ond monðwærust,
leodum liðost   ond lofgeornost.

lament to make, to mourn their king,
chant their dirge, and their chieftain honor.
They praised his earlship, his acts of prowess
worthily witnessed: and well it is
3175
that men their master-friend mightily laud,
heartily love, when hence he goes
from life in the body forlorn away.

Thus made their mourning the men of Geatland,
for their hero's passing his hearth-companions:
3180
quoth that of all the kings of earth,
of men he was mildest and most beloved,
to his kin the kindest, keenest for praise.

{1} Not, of course, Beowulf the Great, hero of the epic.

{2} Kenning for king or chieftain of a comitatus: he breaks off gold from the spiral rings -- often worn on the arm -- and so rewards his followers.

{3} That is, "The Hart," or "Stag," so called from decorations in the gables that resembled the antlers of a deer. This hall has been carefully described in a pamphlet by Heyne. The building was rectangular, with opposite doors -- mainly west and east -- and a hearth in the middle of the single room. A row of pillars down each side, at some distance from the walls, made a space which was raised a little above the main floor, and was furnished with two rows of seats. On one side, usually south, was the high-seat midway between the doors. Opposite this, on the other raised space, was another seat of honor. At the banquet soon to be described, Hrothgar sat in the south or chief high-seat, and Beowulf opposite to him. The scene for a flying was thus very effectively set. Planks on trestles -- the "board" of later English literature --formed the tables just in front of the long rows of seats, and were taken away after banquets, when the retainers were ready to stretch themselves out for sleep on the benches.

{4} Fire was the usual end of these halls. One thinks of the splendid scene at the end of the Nibelungen, of the Nialssaga, of Saxo's story of Amlethus, and many a less famous instance.

{5} It is to be supposed that all hearers of this poem knew how Hrothgar's hall was burnt, -- perhaps in the unsuccessful attack made on him by his son-in-law Ingeld.

{6} A skilled minstrel. The Danes are heathens, as one is told presently; but this lay of beginnings is taken from Genesis.

{7} A disturber of the border, one who sallies from his haunt in the fen and roams over the country near by. This probably pagan nuisance is now furnished with biblical credentials as a fiend or devil in good standing, so that all Christian Englishmen might read about him. "Grendel" may mean one who grinds and crushes.

{8} Cain's.

{9} Giants.

{10} The smaller buildings within the main enclosure but separate from the hall.

{11} Grendel.

{12} "Sorcerers-of-hell."

{13} Hrothgar, who is the "Scyldings'-friend" of 170.

{14} That is, in formal or prescribed phrase.

{15} Ship.

{16} That is, since Beowulf selected his ship and led his men to the harbor.

{17} One of the auxiliary names of the Geats.

{18} Or: Not thus openly ever came warriors hither; yet...

{19} Hrothgar.

{20} Beowulf's helmet has several boar-images on it; he is the "man of war"; and the boar-helmet guards him as typical representative of the marching party as a whole. The boar was sacred to Freyr, who was the favorite god of the Germanic tribes about the North Sea and the Baltic. Rude representations of warriors show the boar on the helmet quite as large as the helmet itself.

{21} Either merely paved, the strata via of the Romans, or else thought of as a sort of mosaic, an extravagant touch like the reckless waste of gold on the walls and roofs of a hall.

{22} The nicor, says Bugge, is a hippopotamus; a walrus, says Ten Brink. But that water-goblin who covers the space from Old Nick of jest to the Neckan and Nix of poetry and tale, is all one needs, and Nicor is a good name for him.

{23} His own people, the Geats.

{24} That is, cover it as with a face-cloth. "There will be no need of funeral rites."

{25} Personification of Battle.

{26} The Germanic Vulcan.

{27} This mighty power, whom the Christian poet can still revere has here the general force of "Destiny."

{28} There is no irrelevance here. Hrothgar sees in Beowulf's mission a heritage of duty, a return of the good offices which the Danish king rendered to Beowulf's father in time of dire need.

{29} Money, for wergild, or man-price.

{30} Ecgtheow, Beowulf's sire.

{31} "Began the fight."

{32} Breca.

{33} Murder.

{34} Beowulf, -- the "one."

{35} That is, he was a "lost soul," doomed to hell.

{36} Kenning for Beowulf.

{37} "Guarded the treasure."

{38} Sc. Heremod.

{39} The singer has sung his lays, and the epic resumes its story. The time-relations are not altogether good in this long passage which describes the rejoicings of "the day after"; but the present shift from the riders on the road to the folk at the hall is not very violent, and is of a piece with the general style.

{40} Unferth, Beowulf's sometime opponent in the flyting.

{41} There is no horrible inconsistency here such as the critics strive and cry about. In spite of the ruin that Grendel and Beowulf had made within the hall, the framework and roof held firm, and swift repairs made the interior habitable. Tapestries were hung on the walls, and willing hands prepared the banquet.

{42} From its formal use in other places, this phrase, to take cup in hall, or "on the floor," would seem to mean that Beowulf stood up to receive his gifts, drink to the donor, and say thanks.

{43} Kenning for sword.

{44} Hrothgar. He is also the "refuge of the friends of Ing, "below. Ing belongs to myth.

{45} Horses are frequently led or ridden into the hall where folk sit at banquet: so in Chaucer's Squire's tale, in the ballad of King Estmere, and in the romances.

{46} Man-price, wergild.

{47} Beowulf's.

{48} Hrothgar.

{49} There is no need to assume a gap in the Ms. As before about Sigemund and Heremod, so now, though at greater length, about Finnand his feud, a lay is chanted or recited; and the epic poet, counting on his readers' familiarity with the story, -- a fragment of it still exists, -- simply gives the headings.

{50} The exact story to which this episode refers in summary is not to be determined, but the following account of it is reasonable and has good support among scholars. Finn, a Frisian chieftain, who nevertheless has a "castle" outside the Frisian border, marries Hildeburh, a Danish princess; and her brother, Hnaef, with many other Danes, pays Finn a visit. Relations between the two peoples have been strained before. Something starts the old feud anew; and the visitors are attacked in their quarters. Hnaef is killed; so is a son of Hildeburh. Many fall on both sides. Peace is patched up; a stately funeral is held; and the surviving visitors become in a way vassals or liegemen of Finn, going back with him to Frisia. So matters rest a while. Hengest is now leader of the Danes; but he is set upon revenge for his former lord, Hnaef.

Probably he is killed in feud; but his clansmen, Guthlaf and Oslaf, gather at their home a force of sturdy Danes, come back to Frisia, storm Finn's stronghold, kill him, and carry back their kinswoman Hildeburh.

{51} The "enemies" must be the Frisians.

{52} Battlefield. -- Hengest is the "prince's thane," companion of Hnaef. "Folcwald's son" is Finn.

{53} That is, Finn would govern in all honor the few Danish warriors who were left, provided, of course, that none of them tried to renew the quarrel or avenge Hnaef their fallen lord. If, again, one of Finn's Frisians began a quarrel, he should die by the sword.

{54} Hnaef.

{55} The high place chosen for the funeral: see description of Beowulf's funeral-pile at the end of the poem.

{56} Wounds.

{57} That is, these two Danes, escaping home, had told the story of the attack on Hnaef, the slaying of Hengest, and all the Danish woes. Collecting a force, they return to Frisia and kill Finn in his home.

{58} Nephew to Hrothgar, with whom he subsequently quarrels, and elder cousin to the two young sons of Hrothgar and Wealhtheow, --their natural guardian in the event of the king's death. There is something finely feminine in this speech of Wealhtheow's, apart from its somewhat irregular and irrelevant sequence of topics. Both she and her lord probably distrust Hrothulf; but she bids the king to be of good cheer, and, turning to the suspect, heaps affectionate assurances on his probity. "My own Hrothulf" will surely not forget these favors and benefits of the past, but will repay them to the orphaned boy.

{59} They had laid their arms on the benches near where they slept.

{60} He surmises presently where she is.

{61} The connection is not difficult. The words of mourning, of acute grief, are said; and according to Germanic sequence oft thought, inexorable here, the next and only topic is revenge. But is it possible? Hrothgar leads up to his appeal and promise with a skillful and often effective description of the horrors which surround the monster's home and await the attempt of an avenging foe.

{62} Hrothgar is probably meant.

{63} Meeting place.

{64} Kenning for "sword." Hrunting is bewitched, laid under a spell of uselessness, along with all other swords.

{65} This brown of swords, evidently meaning burnished, bright, continues to be a favorite adjective in the popular ballads.

{66} After the killing of the monster and Grendel's decapitation.

{67} Hrothgar.

{68} The blade slowly dissolves in blood-stained drops like icicles.

{69} Spear.

{70} That is, "whoever has as wide authority as I have and can remember so far back so many instances of heroism, may well say, as I say, that no better hero ever lived than Beowulf."

{71} That is, he is now undefended by conscience from the temptations (shafts) of the devil.

{72} Kenning for the sun. -- This is a strange role for the raven. He is the warrior's bird of battle, exults in slaughter and carnage; his joy here is a compliment to the sunrise.

{73} That is, he might or might not see Beowulf again. Old as he was, the latter chance was likely; but he clung to the former, hoping to see his young friend again "and exchange brave words in the hall."

{74} With the speed of the boat.

{75} Queen to Hygelac. She is praised by contrast with the antitype, Thryth, just as Beowulf was praised by contrast with Heremod.

{76} Kenning for "wife."

{77} Beowulf gives his uncle the king not mere gossip of his journey, but a statesmanlike forecast of the outcome of certain policies at the Danish court. Talk of interpolation here is absurd. As both Beowulf and Hygelac know, -- and the folk for whom the Beowulf was put together also knew, -- Froda was king of the Heathobards (probably the Langobards, once near neighbors of Angle and Saxon tribes on the continent), and had fallen in fight with the Danes. Hrothgar will set aside this feud by giving his daughter as "peace-weaver" and wife to the young king Ingeld, son of the slain Froda. But Beowulf, on general principles and from his observation of the particular case, foretells trouble. Note:

{78} Play of shields, battle. A Danish warrior cuts down Froda in the fight, and takes his sword and armor, leaving them to a son. This son is selected to accompany his mistress, the young princess Freawaru, to her new home when she is Ingeld's queen. Heedlessly he wears the sword of Froda in hall. An old warrior points it out to Ingeld, and eggs him on to vengeance. At his instigation the Dane is killed; but the murderer, afraid of results, and knowing the land, escapes. So the old feud must break out again.

{79} That is, their disastrous battle and the slaying of their king.

{80} The sword.

{81} Beowulf returns to his forecast. Things might well go some what as follows, he says; sketches a little tragic story; and with this prophecy by illustration returns to the tale of his adventure.

{82} Not an actual glove, but a sort of bag.

{83} Hygelac.

{84} This is generally assumed to mean hides, though the text simply says "seven thousand." A hide in England meant about 120 acres, though "the size of the acre varied."

{84} On the historical raid into Frankish territory between 512 and 520 A.D. The subsequent course of events, as gathered from hints of this epic, is partly told in Scandinavian legend.

{86} The chronology of this epic, as scholars have worked it out, would make Beowulf well over ninety years of age when he fights the dragon. But the fifty years of his reign need not be taken as historical fact.

{87} The text is here hopelessly illegible, and only the general drift of the meaning can be rescued. For one thing, we have the old myth of a dragon who guards hidden treasure. But with this runs the story of some noble, last of his race, who hides all his wealth within this barrow and there chants his farewell to life's glories. After his death the dragon takes possession of the hoard and watches over it. A condemned or banished man, desperate, hides in the barrow, discovers the treasure, and while the dragon sleeps, makes off with a golden beaker or the like, and carries it for propitiation to his master. The dragon discovers the loss and exacts fearful penalty from the people round about.

{88} Literally "loan-days," days loaned to man.

{89} Chattuarii, a tribe that dwelt along the Rhine, and took part in repelling the raid of (Hygelac) Chocilaicus.

{90} Onela, son of Ongentheow, who pursues his two nephews Eanmund and Eadgils to Heardred's court, where they have taken refuge after their unsuccessful rebellion. In the fighting Heardred is killed.

{91} That is, Beowulf supports Eadgils against Onela, who is slainby Eadgils in revenge for the "care-paths" of exile into which Onela forced him.

{92} That is, the king could claim no wergild, or man-price, from one son for the killing of the other.

{93} Usual euphemism for death.

{94} Sc. in the grave.

{95} Eofor for Wulf. -- The immediate provocation for Eofor in killing "the hoary Scylfing," Ongentheow, is that the latter has just struck Wulf down; but the king, Haethcyn, is also avenged bythe blow. See the detailed description below.

{96} Hygelac.

{97} Shield.

{98} The hollow passage.

{99} That is, although Eanmund was brother's son to Onela, the slaying of the former by Weohstan is not felt as cause of feud, and is rewarded by gift of the slain man's weapons.

{100} Both Wiglaf and the sword did their duty. -- The following is one of the classic passages for illustrating the comitatus as the most conspicuous Germanic institution, and its underlying sense of duty, based partly on the idea of loyalty and partly on the practical basis of benefits received and repaid.

{101} Sc. "than to bide safely here," -- a common figure of incomplete comparison.

{102} Wiglaf's wooden shield.

{103} Gering would translate "kinsman of the nail," as both are made of iron.

{104} That is, swords.

{105} Where Beowulf lay.

{106} What had been left or made by the hammer; well-forged.

{107} Trying to revive him.

{108} Nothing.

{109} Dead.

{110} Death-watch, guard of honor, "lyke-wake."

{111} A name for the Franks.

{112} Ongentheow.

{113} Haethcyn.

{114} The line may mean: till Hrethelings stormed on the hedgedshields, -- i.e. the shield-wall or hedge of defensive war --Hrethelings, of course, are Geats.

{115} Eofor, brother to Wulf Wonreding.

{116} Sc. "value in" hides and the weight of the gold.

{117} Not at all.

{118} Laid on it when it was put in the barrow. This spell, or in our days the "curse," either prevented discovery or brought dire ills on the finder and taker.

{119} Probably the fugitive is meant who discovered the hoard. Ten Brink and Gering assume that the dragon is meant. "Hid" may well mean here "took while in hiding."

{120} That is "one and a few others." But Beowulf seems to be indicated.

{121} Ten Brink points out the strongly heathen character of this part of the epic. Beowulf's end came, so the old tradition ran, from his unwitting interference with spell-bound treasure.

{122} A hard saying, variously interpreted. In any case, it is the somewhat clumsy effort of the Christian poet to tone down the heathenism of his material by an edifying observation.

{123} Nothing is said of Beowulf's wife in the poem, but Bugge surmises that Beowulf finally accepted Hygd's offer of kingdom and hoard, and, as was usual, took her into the bargain.

CPSIA information can be obtained
at www.ICGtesting.com
Printed in the USA
LVOW10s2252011017
550808LV00001B/20/P